THE LONDON MURDER MYSTERIES

The DEADLY FIRE

CORA HARRISON

PICCADILLY PRESS • LONDON

For Noah, Peter, Abe, Alexander,
Joel and Reuben

First published in Great Britain in 2010
by Piccadilly Press Ltd,
5 Castle Road, London NW1 8PR
www.piccadillypress.co.uk

A catalogue record for this book is available
from the British Library

ISBN: 978 1 84812 082 2 (paperback)

1 3 5 7 9 10 8 6 4 2

Printed in the UK by CPI Bookmarque, Croydon, CR0 4TD
Cover design by Patrick Knowles
Cover illustration by Chris King

CHAPTER 1

THE
BETRAYAL

Alfie gulped nervously and looked around. Night was falling and the fog was thicker and more yellow than ever. One by one, the costermongers were blowing out the torches in their stalls. The unsold fruit and vegetables had been packed into carts and wheeled away. Soon the entire square would be emptied of people. Those who were still there turned their gaze away uneasily from the sight of a twelve-year-old boy in the vicious grip of the most feared and hated person in the whole of Covent Garden market.

Mary Robinson, known as the Queen of the Costermongers, was the tallest, widest, strongest woman that Alfie had ever known. She always dressed in a man's overcoat and a man's hat, and under her calf-length gown she wore a pair of men's trousers. Her voice was like a man's also, deep and hoarse, and she had the strength of the strongest dock labourer. Now she took hold of Alfie and shook him, knocking his head against the wooden struts of a nearby stall until he began to see stars in the fog surrounding him.

'I've got you now,' she hissed, holding his throat with one large rough hand while rummaging in his pocket with the other. 'So it's you that's been spreading this poison among the stallholders, you pestilent little beast. Don't think that I don't know where you live, neither!' She had taken the leaflets from his pocket, screwed them viciously into the shape of a corkscrew and thrust it at him like an accusing finger. Alfie knew what was printed on them.

*DO NOT ALLOW MARY ROBINSON
TO CHEAT YOU.
SHE LENDS YOU EIGHT HALF-CROWNS
ON MONDAY.
SHE TAKES BACK NINE HALF-CROWNS
ON SATURDAY.*

MARY ROBINSON MAKES
A FORTUNE EVERY YEAR
WHILE YOU AND YOUR CHILDREN
STARVE.

'I'll kill you,' she spat. 'I mean it. No one will miss a slum kid like you. It's going to be a frosty night tonight – your body won't be the only one to be swept up by the street cleaners in the morning and no questions asked. Come on, answer my question. Who got those leaflets printed? Don't tell me any lies, neither. I've my fingers on your throat and you wouldn't be the first that I have choked the life out of.'

She was in earnest, this Mary Robinson. Alfie knew that. He cast a quick, desperate glance around to see if his cousins Tom and Jack were near, but no one was around except his blind brother, Sammy. Sammy sang for the stallholders and their customers, and charitable people put a few coppers into the bowl at his feet. Now, however, there was no one left to sing for, and Sammy waited patiently for Alfie to lead him home.

The woman saw his glance and Alfie heard her chuckle. 'And he's your little brother, isn't he?

Perhaps I'll choke the life out of him first. Let you watch him die! Have you ever heard a man die from strangulation? I have, and I'll tell you that it's not an easy death. A boy would be quicker, but he'll suffer just as much.'

And then she was walking over towards Sammy, dragging Alfie along, her hard fingers still at his throat, the first finger and thumb pressing in so that he could not yell, could not even whisper, could not warn Sammy, could not tell him to run. Desperately, he reached up and clawed at her hand.

'I'll tell you,' he managed to say, his breath wheezing like that of an old man.

'That's better. Seeing a bit of sense, are you?' Her grip eased a little, just a very little, just enough so that he could gasp out the name.

'Mr Elmore!'

'Who's Mr Elmore?' Once again the grip tightened warningly before release.

'He's the teacher. The teacher at the Ragged School, at St Giles.'

'I know him. The son of the goldsmith in Ludgate Hill, son of a rich man. So that's who is trying to rob a poor woman like me! Well, Mr Elmore won't see you again, and he won't see that blind brother of

4

yours neither. He'll just be a burden on the parish when you're dead, so I'll get rid of him as well as you.'

And then Alfie knew that it was all over. He had betrayed Mr Elmore for no reason. He was still going to die and so was Sammy. He had broken his promise to his dead mother to look after his blind brother. That was his last thought as the life was slowly squeezed out of him and a deadly faintness came over him.

CHAPTER 2

SHOOT
THAT DOG!

And then there was a whistle. A sharp, high whistle and then a note: just one note. A note pitched almost impossibly high. A boy's voice. Sammy's. His whistle, too. Sammy could not see, but his hearing was pin-sharp. He knew that Alfie was in danger and he had called for help.

Then a bark. A deep bark. A scrabble of paws on the cobbled surface of Covent Garden. A shout of warning from one of the costermongers. Another bark, a whole series of barks and then, from deep down in the chest of a large dog, an angry growl.

The grip on Alfie's neck slackened. He opened his

eyes. Mary Robinson was no longer holding him. She wasn't even looking at him. She was staring fearfully ahead.

'Help!' she screamed. One of her helpers approached with a torch and then another. The pitch on the torches flamed up and lit the scene.

It was Mutsy! Faithful Mutsy. Mutsy, who had followed Alfie home one day from Smithfield market to make his home with the four orphan boys and to love and protect them. He was a very large, very hairy dog with enormous paws and a heavy fringe of hair hanging down, a dog who made most people smile, but there was nothing comic about him now. Every fibre of his body bristled with menace.

Step by step, he advanced on Mary Robinson. Each hair of his coat seemed to be standing on end, making his body appear almost twice as big as normal. His brown eyes, usually so soft and loving, were now hard, and fixed on Mary Robinson's face. His lips were stripped back from his teeth.

Pace by pace, his huge paws moved threateningly across the ground.

'Help!' screamed Mary Robinson again. 'Police! Help!' Her loud harsh voice rang through the square. She let go of Alfie. Quickly, she snatched a torch from one of the men and threatened Mutsy with it. The big dog did not flinch, though. Still he growled, standing so close to his owner that Alfie could feel heat from Mutsy's body against his bare leg.

'Police! Help!' screamed Mary Robinson once more and this time there was an answering shrill sound of the police whistle. A few of the people standing around disappeared, but most stayed.

Alfie put a hand on Mutsy's back and looked over at Sammy. Was there any way that he could get himself and his brother away from this place? He took a hesitant step backwards, but Mary Robinson flourished the torch again, and Mutsy growled and snapped at her.

'Kill that dog! Shoot him! He's mad. He has rabies! He tried to attack me. Everyone saw him. Listen to him growl,' she screamed at the breathless policeman who had just arrived, still blowing on the small whistle attached to his uniform.

'I haven't got a gun, ma'am,' said the policeman diffidently. He probably knew Mary Robinson. He sounded scared of the woman.

'Well, hit him with your truncheon, then. What do we have policemen for if they can't defend us against a mad dog?' Mary Robinson looked around at the crowd, inviting them to agree with her.

The policeman took one tentative step towards Mutsy, swinging his truncheon in a half-hearted way. Mutsy glanced at him, then settled his gaze back on Mary Robinson and gave another ferocious growl.

The policeman blew his whistle again. 'I'll have to get the dog catcher, ma'am. He's got a net and he can kill the dog when he's safely trapped in the net.'

'He's not mad. He was trying to defend me and my blind brother,' croaked Alfie, his throat so sore that he could hardly speak. He kept his hand on Mutsy's collar and moved cautiously over to join Sammy. Now the three of them were together and his courage came back to him. 'That woman tried to strangle me,' he said, bravely pointing at Mary Robinson.

'You little . . .' Mary Robinson took two steps towards him, and then backed away hastily as Mutsy showed his teeth and growled again.

'Here's another peeler,' shouted one of the coster-mongers as a second policeman came panting up through the crowd.

'We want a dog catcher,' bawled the first police-man. 'There's a mad dog here.'

'The dog's not mad,' repeated Alfie. His voice was beginning to come back, though his throat was still very sore. To his relief, he could see a familiar face above the navy-blue uniform and the number on his collar. 'You know me, PC 29. Inspector Denham knows me – Alfie Sykes from Bow Street.'

The second policeman hesitated. A glance passed between him and his colleague and then he nodded. He spoke in a low voice, but Alfie could hear the words 'Runs errands for Inspector Denham'.

Cautiously, he drew in a deep breath. 'Is it all right if I take my brother home out of this freezing fog, sir?' He did not look at Mary Robinson, but addressed the first policeman with as much politeness as he could manage to get into his croaking voice.

Once again the two policemen exchanged glances and then the first said, with a jerk of his head, 'Go on; hop it!'

Thankfully, Alfie seized his blind brother's hand and put his other on the rope collar around Mutsy's neck. As he made his way towards the edge of Covent Garden Square, he could see his two cousins waiting for him.

'What happened?' asked Jack.

'Mutsy just took off when I was doing a trick with him,' complained Tom, Jack's younger brother.

Alfie opened his mouth to answer, but closed it again. Someone had tapped him on the back and then thrust a piece of paper into his hand. Alfie looked at it curiously. It was one of the leaflets that he had been handing out, the leaflet that Mr Elmore of the Ragged School had printed in an effort to stop the coster-mongers being robbed by Mary Robinson.

The back of the paper should have been blank, but this one had something drawn on it.

It was the picture of a boy – crudely and badly drawn with a piece of charred wood from a torch. But that was not all.

The boy in the picture had a rope around his neck and he dangled from a gallows.

Alfie drew in a long breath and felt his heart thump wildly.

There was no mistaking the meaning of Mary Robinson's message.

CHAPTER 3

THE BODY SNATCHER

'Stop arguing, Tom. I say you go to school, and you go to school.'

Alfie had had a hard day and his throat still ached from Mary Robinson's fingers. He spoke angrily: he was tired of Tom. They had this argument every single night. Tom did not enjoy the Ragged School. He was finding it almost impossible to learn his letters and he was still in the lowest class in the school. Alfie bent over the fire in the cellar they called their home, carefully dampening it down with a mixture of coal dust and water. No sense in wasting fuel while they were all out.

'I could stay at home with Sammy if you're worried

about that Mary Robinson,' grumbled Tom for the tenth time as the four of them made their way down Monmouth Street. 'Me and Mutsy – we wouldn't let nobody in. You could trust us. You'll only get into trouble bringing a blind boy and a dog to school.'

'Shut up,' said Alfie. Mary Robinson's remark about knowing where he lived lingered in his mind. He knew there was some truth in what Tom said. He didn't think that Mr Elmore would mind him bringing Sammy. Sammy was quick and sharp and even if he couldn't see, he could join in the chanting of the alphabet with everyone in the first class. No, it wasn't Sammy he was worried about – it was Mutsy. Even a man as kind as Mr Elmore might refuse to have a dog in his school.

On the other hand, Alfie did not want to walk through the dark, fog-filled streets without Mutsy's protection. He wasn't just scared of Mary Robinson and her gang of toughs – it was said in the market that some of those fellows would knife a man as quickly as they would cut a cabbage stalk – but she was not the only menace that stalked the gas-lit streets of this part of London.

Alfie caught his breath in a gasp of fear as he saw a burly figure approaching them from the direction of the Drury Lane burying ground.

Joseph Bishop was feared and loathed by all. Even the poorest of the poor – even people who rented one corner of a room in the crazy, tumbledown houses in the parish of St Giles – would not do what Joseph Bishop did.

He was a grave robber, a body snatcher.

In the darkness of the night, even in the dim twilight of foggy days, Joseph Bishop went into the burying ground of Drury Lane and dug up bodies which he sold to the medical students at St Bart's Hospital for dissection. But, even worse, people said that he also murdered children to sell their bodies. Perhaps it was easier to kill a child than to dig one up from the stinking earth of the over-crowded burying ground.

'Keep well out of his way,' Mr Elmore had warned a week before. He had looked all around the room, making sure that every child in his Ragged School was listening to him, before continuing. 'There was a young boy who used to come here, a boy with a twisted leg. The last that anyone saw of him, he was talking to Joseph Bishop. I have spoken to the police about this, but nothing is done. It seems as if only the murders of the rich and the powerful are investigated by them.'

Alfie had known what Mr Elmore meant. Ever since then he had kept a sharp eye on Sammy. Perhaps the body of a blind boy would be of interest to the medical students.

'Ugh,' muttered Tom now, pinching his nose between his finger and thumb, as Joseph Bishop approached them.

'Shut up,' muttered Alfie. Tom had no sense. His older brother Jack was quiet and easy-going – a loyal member of the gang and a hard worker, but Tom was a trouble-maker, always rebelling against Alfie's rule and challenging every decision.

Joseph Bishop looked at the four boys narrowly as he passed, transferring a sack of something bulky and evil-smelling from one shoulder to the other. He said nothing, though – just looked at them, then at Mutsy, and then passed on. A deep growl rumbled in Mutsy's chest, but it was low and Alfie covered it by exclaiming quickly, 'There's Sarah!'

'Hello, Sarah,' said Tom.

'Why are you looking so glum, Tom?' Sarah asked, and Tom scowled.

'You're late, Sarah,' said Jack hurriedly with an eye on his brother's annoyed face. 'You're usually at the school before the door even opens.'

Sarah was the scullery maid in one of the posh houses in Bloomsbury Street, just to the north of the parish of St Giles. The mistress at her previous house had overheard Sammy singing in the streets and had got her coachman to bring him back to her drawing room to sing there. Sarah had taken Sammy home to the cellar afterwards and had made friends with the other boys. She, Alfie and the rest of the gang had worked together in solving the murder of Mr Montgomery for Inspector Denham. The puzzle could not have been worked out if Sarah had not been able to read and that made Alfie determined that he, Jack and Tom would also learn.

'Is Sammy coming to school, too?' Sarah sounded surprised as she stroked Mutsy.

'I just thought I'd bring Sammy along,' said Alfie in an off-hand manner. 'I had a bit of trouble today – with Mary Robinson.'

'Those leaflets that Mr Elmore got printed!' Sarah had a quick, clever brain.

'That's right. That woman tried to strangle me.' Alfie stopped under a gas lamp, tilted his chin and showed the black bruises on his throat. 'She threatened Sammy, too. She said that she knew where we lived so I thought I would bring him with us.' He didn't

16

mention Mutsy; he didn't like to admit that he felt uneasy about walking through the streets of St Giles without the presence of his faithful dog. In every shadow he seemed to see the huge, burly form of Mary Robinson, dressed in a man's overcoat and a man's hat.

'Coward,' taunted Tom. 'You nearly wet yourself, didn't you, just because a woman gave you a shaking! Can't think of nothing else but Mary Robinson, Mary Robinson, Mary Robinson! He's been going on about her for the last hour or so, Sarah. He's scared stiff, poor little boy!'

'You shut up or I'll make you sorry,' retorted Alfie. He doubled his fists, but then uncurled them reluctantly. He didn't want to upset Jack. Jack was such a good friend as well as a cousin, never complaining, always ready to do the worst jobs like spending freezing hours up to his knees in the filthy water of the Thames, searching for pieces of coal. Without Jack, their life in the damp cellar in Bow Street would be a lot less comfortable. His brother just had to be put up with.

Without saying a word, Alfie walked on. A flood of bad language was coming from Tom, but Alfie ignored it. Tom wasn't too bright; he would soon run out of things to say and then they could forget their quarrel.

'Come on, Tom,' said Jack, the peacemaker, after a few minutes. 'Cheer up.'

'Well, I'm tired of him bossing me. Who's he to say that I should waste my evenings going to school?' Tom moodily kicked a stone from the pavement right under the feet of a passing horse.

'Give it another try,' advised Jack. 'It will come to you all of a sudden, you'll find.'

'We'll probably all be turned out anyway, what with Alfie dragging Sammy and Mutsy along,' said Tom. Typically, he sounded quite good-humoured, now.

Alfie didn't turn his head. He had worse things to worry him than Tom. His eyes were fixed on the tall, broad figure emerging abruptly from a darkened doorway and then striding away from them, rounding the corner towards Great Russell Street.

He met Sarah's eyes and said in a low voice, 'I think that might have been Mary Robinson.'

CHAPTER 4

THE SCHOOL

The Ragged School in Streatham Street was the last of the old houses built hundreds of years before, when St Giles was just a village outside London. Its ancient wooden frame had begun to rot away, and it lurched to one side, looking as though it would fall down any day in a gust of wind, or just sink back into the mud around it. Inside, it had a stone floor with two rooms downstairs and a large walk-in cupboard beside the front door. A crazily leaning wooden staircase led up to three more rooms.

Mr Elmore, a small, heavily bearded figure, dressed as usual in a slightly shabby black frock coat and close-fitting black trousers, was at the door when they arrived.

'Come in,' he said with a warm smile at Sarah, who was one of his star pupils. 'And who is this?'

He had seen at a glance that Sammy was blind and he took his hand with such gentleness that Alfie felt doubly ashamed to think how he had betrayed this kind man.

'This is Sammy, my brother,' he said. 'I'm a bit worried . . .' He gulped a bit and decided not to mention the name of Mary Robinson. 'I thought you might not mind if I brought him along,' he finished.

'Come and learn your ABC, Sammy,' said Mr Elmore gently. He ushered them into the big room to the right of the front door, saying, 'You're very welcome to our school.' He eyed Mutsy with a slight smile. 'And what about this fellow? Can he read yet?'

'I thought we might need him on the street. He's a good dog to protect us. I'm a bit worried . . .' Once again Alfie lapsed into silence and Mr Elmore gave an understanding nod.

'Tell me about it later. First, let's get these two settled into class.'

The alphabet class was conducted by one of the monitors, a tall, skinny boy called Albert. Like the other monitors, he had already learned to read and write and was paid sixpence a week to teach the other children. Mr Elmore introduced Sammy to Albert and told him that Mutsy would be staying too. Albert looked surprised, but grinned as Mr Elmore said, 'He seems a good dog.'

Mutsy gave an extra wag of the tail in appreciation of this kindness and sat down beside Sammy and Tom.

The other pupils came crowding in a few minutes later. After a quick stare at Sammy and Mutsy, they took their places on the three battered benches that lined the room. Each bench seated six and Albert stood in front of them and started to sing the alphabet song which they all joined in with cheerfully.

Sammy was quick and clever, used to learning songs, and he rapidly picked up the chant of the twenty-six letters of the alphabet. Mr Elmore smiled appreciatively as he heard Sammy's clear, high, beautiful voice soaring up with the words, *And now I know my ABC* . . . He left the monitor to instruct the rest of the class in fitting letters together to make *DOG*, *CAT* and other three-letter words while he took Sammy to the back of the room, asking him to sing song after song.

'You have a rare gift here,' he said, patting Sammy on the shoulder. 'I wish that I had the money to pay for lessons for you. However . . .' He stopped and thought for a moment and then smiled.

'I know a man in Ludgate Hill who loves music and has more money than he knows what to do with,' he went on. 'I'll have a word with him and see what he can do.'

Sammy smiled a smile of sheer joy but Alfie, waiting patiently until Mr Elmore was free to hear about Mary Robinson, felt a pang of fear that this hope would be disappointed.

'Why should this rich man in Ludgate Hill be interested in what you say about Sammy?' he asked harshly.

'Because he is my father,' said Mr Elmore. 'Now tell me how you got on with those leaflets.'

'Can we go up into your office?' asked Alfie nervously. He was worried about the other children listening in, but also his feeling of shame at having betrayed the teacher's name made him reluctant to begin his story.

Mr Elmore's office was a small room crammed with books. It had only one tiny window high up in the wall and the floorboards were badly broken in places. In one corner was a rickety, worm-eaten desk with the remains of a couple of loaves of bread on it. Any hungry pupil was welcome to some of the teacher's supper before or after lessons.

Mr Elmore brushed Alfie's excuses aside and did not seem to be worried about the threat to him. His face darkened, however, when he heard the full account of the attack on Alfie and the threat to Sammy.

'I'll go straight down to Bow Street police station tomorrow morning,' he said decisively. 'We have a perfect right to tell these unfortunate costermongers the truth. She won't get away with this again. I plan to distribute leaflets in all of the markets in London where that woman operates. These are for Smithfield, these for Petticoat Lane, these for Leadenhall and for Newgate.' He nodded at the separate piles of leaflets on his desk. Alfie felt his heart sink as he gazed at them. He had no desire to meet Mary Robinson again. He looked from the leaflets to Mr Elmore and found that the man was smiling.

'Don't worry, boy, I wouldn't ask you again. Now get on with your work, Alfie. You are making very good progress. I think you will probably be finished with the writing class this week and then I'll move you up to the third class and you can study spelling there. Keep up the reading practice. Every time you see a piece of print, try to get its meaning. We'll have you reading your Bible before long. Now don't you worry about Mary Robinson. I'll get the Bow Street runners on her tail.'

Alfie nodded and left the room, bumping into Tom outside the door. 'What are you doing here?' he snapped. 'No wonder you can't learn if you don't stay in your own classroom.' It was a relief to lose his temper with Tom, but Alfie felt slightly ashamed of himself when his cousin turned without a word and stomped down the stairs.

Back in the classroom, Alfie practised his hand-writing, still worrying about Mary Robinson, despite Mr Elmore's words. He had a feeling that Bow Street police station would not take too much notice of the teacher. Even if he were a toff, the eldest son of a rich goldsmith, he had chosen to spend his life working with the poorest of the poor children of London.

Mr Elmore wasn't like any other toff he had ever met, Alfie thought to himself as he dipped his quill pen into the ink pot. The Ragged School and its pupils seemed to be the most important thing in his life. He had dismissed a teacher, Thomas Orrack, because he had been violent towards the children. He had refused to allow the terrible building to be pulled down and houses for the rich to be built on the spot.

'You're wasting your time,' Alfie had heard a gentleman in a frock coat and tall hat say to Mr Elmore a few months ago. 'There will come a time when the whole of St Giles will be pulled down. You might as well give in now.'

'I bought this building and it's mine to do what I like with, and what I like is to teach the poor unfortunate children of St Giles to read and write.' The whole school had heard their teacher yell those words.

'You didn't take those leaflets from my desk, did you?' Mr Elmore suddenly appeared at Alfie's shoulder, making him jump.

'Take the leaflets? No, I never.' Not likely, thought Alfie. He had had enough of Mary Robinson and would be glad never to hear her name again.

'Odd! They seem to have disappeared.' Mr Elmore thought about it for a moment and then seemed to dismiss the matter from his mind. 'Your brother, Sammy, is a bright boy,' he continued. 'I've got an idea for teaching him to read. I read in a book about a man called Braille who invented a touch-system that is used to teach the blind. He'll need to know his letters first, though, and how the letters join together to make the words. I was just thinking that if we could get some clay from the brickworks, some of the children in the alphabet class could make him some letters so that he could feel the shape and then learn the sound. Just run down there, Alfie, will you? Tell the foreman that I know Mr Lambert, the property developer. You could say he and I are great friends – he comes to see me often enough! Anyway, say that I'm sure that Mr Lambert would want to please me. We only need enough clay to make a brick.'

Alfie got slowly to his feet. He was reluctant to leave his work. He gazed with admiration at the page of perfect copperplate handwriting that he had produced. He had just got the hang of the mystery, he thought. Suddenly all of those squiggles that surrounded him were beginning to make sense. He had learned to read print and now he was learning to write and to read other people's handwriting. He could talk to people without a word being spoken by anyone.

'Couldn't Tom go?' he asked.

'Can't find Tom anywhere,' said Mr Elmore

dismissively. 'He has a bad habit of wandering from class to class. I scolded him earlier when I saw him coming out of my office so now he is probably sulking. Go on, like a good lad. Between us we might start teaching your blind brother to read this very evening.'

CHAPTER 5

THE
BRICKWORKS

The brickworks were busy when Alfie arrived. They worked past midnight there, Alfie knew, turning out the bricks to build the new houses in Bloomsbury. Clay was everywhere. Piles and piles of it were being thumped by children as young as seven or eight. From time to time the foreman came up and tested a piece, and, if all the air had not been wedged out, the child got thumped. He seemed to be a bad-tempered man who was continually shouting at everyone.

Alfie put on his politest voice. 'Mr Elmore, from the Ragged School, asked if you could give me a slab of clay. He said that he knows Mr Lambert and that he was sure that Mr Lambert would not refuse him.'

'Well, Mr Lambert isn't here now,' sneered the foreman. 'I don't think you would expect to find a man like that working at this hour of the night. He's probably at home eating a ten-course dinner in his posh house.'

'He's rich, then, is he?' Alfie was always curious about people.

The foreman snorted. 'Rich! Of course he is rich! What do you think? He has built half the houses around here and plans to build more. Go on, get out of here and stop wasting my time.' Then his face changed. 'Good evening, Mr Lambert. Didn't expect to see you here at this hour of the night, Mr Lambert.'

Alfie immediately recognised Mr Lambert as the man in the frock coat who had made Mr Elmore lose his temper. He was a small man with a large stomach, quite round in shape, and with a smiling face. He had approached them very quietly and Alfie was fairly sure that he must have overheard the foreman's words.

'Who's this young man?' he asked mildly.

'Sent by Mr Elmore from the Ragged School, sir,' said the foreman nervously. 'Wants some clay, sir. Said that you would give him some.'

Mr Lambert laughed pleasantly. 'Are you one of his prize pupils?' he asked genially. 'Go on, we can spare some clay for such a good man as Mr Elmore. Let him take what he wants,' he said to the foreman.

Alfie waited until Mr Lambert walked away, stumbling slightly on the uneven ground, and then he found a flat piece of wood and piled plenty of clay on to it. He didn't think it would matter how much he took. Tons of the stuff was being pressed into moulds, then tipped out on to boards, carried to the kiln, baked and put out to cool.

By the time that Alfie arrived back at the school, his arms aching from the heavy load of clay, he was half sorry that he had taken so much – about four times as much as Mr Elmore had told him to get.

He pushed open the front door and stood in the hallway for a moment.

'What you got there?' asked Albert, who was busy filling the inkpots from a large bottle of black ink that lived in the large, walk-in cupboard beside the front door.

'Mr Elmore wanted some clay, but I've got much too much,' explained Alfie, looking ruefully at the enormous lump on the piece of board. 'Perhaps I should throw half of it away. What do you think?'

'Don't do that,' said Albert. 'You'd never know, it might come in useful. Put it in here.' He surveyed the cupboard and stared dubiously at the rickety shelves, stacked with old slates, broken pieces of chalk, offcuts of paper and a few quill pens.

'Best put it on the floor,' he decided and watched while Alfie put the large wet lump of clay on the cupboard floor.

When Alfie came into the alphabet class with the rest of the clay, Mr Elmore was still with Sammy, fascinated by the speed with which the blind boy was learning. He seemed to be the brightest pupil in the first class. Mr Elmore had taken out some letter cards, and Alfie rubbed long worms of clay between his hands and bent them to cover the letters.

Mr Elmore was teaching Sammy words beginning with the letter D.

'Doctor, dig,' said Mr Elmore. 'Down, desperate, dirt, disease, despair, destroy . . .'

'Dog,' said Sammy with a grin and a quick pat of Mutsy, who was sitting bolt upright beside him, looking intelligent and alert.

Quickly Alfie arranged the letters *DOG* on a small tray and handed them to Sammy, helping him to trace the shape of the three letters. Sammy's face lit up as he understood. Alfie grinned and showed the tray to Mutsy, barely forming the word 'Bark' with his lips, and Mutsy barked.

Then Alfie made *RAT*, allowed Sammy to feel the three letters and then, in a whisper as low as a sigh, said 'Growl' to Mutsy and Mutsy growled.

At the end of school time, Mr Elmore brought the whole school into the big room downstairs to see the fun. Over fifty children were standing around laughing as time after time Alfie tested Mutsy. Every time Mutsy saw the word *DOG* he barked and wagged his tail, and every time he saw the word *RAT* he growled and stripped his teeth.

'Make a great new trick, this. We should earn some more money with the reading dog,' said Jack and looked around for Tom to share the joke.

But there was no sign of Tom anywhere and now school was finishing for the evening.

Tom had been missing for over two hours.

Where had he gone?

The figure of Joseph Bishop flashed through Alfie's mind.

CHAPTER 6

FIRE!

'Oh!' exclaimed Sarah.

'What's the matter?' asked Sammy. Alfie said nothing; he was too busy scanning the crowd in St Giles High Street, looking for Tom. Jack, he noticed, was doing the same thing with a worried look on his freckled face.

'I've left my key behind,' explained Sarah. 'I took it out of my pocket because Mr Elmore asked us to write about an everyday object and I forgot to put it back when I had finished describing it.'

'We'll go back – Mr Elmore will probably still be there,' said Alfie. In a way, he was glad of an excuse not to go home. What was he going to do if Tom was not there when they arrived back at the cellar in Bow Street? He and Jack would have to go out again and look for him. But what about Sammy? He didn't fancy dragging his blind brother around the midnight streets of St Giles. He didn't fancy any of them being out with the menace of Joseph Bishop or Mary Robinson hanging over them!

'Let's go quickly,' he said decisively, setting such a fast pace that after a few minutes, he and Sarah were well ahead of Jack, Sammy and Mutsy.

The fog was very dense that night; even the gas lamps in the High Street were dimmed by it. But when they turned the corner, they stopped in amazement.

Streatham Street had no gas lamps, but the whole street was bathed in a red-gold radiance lighting up one of the windows of the Ragged School.

And there was a strange smell. Not the usual stench of rotting filth. A sharp smell, a scorching, smoking, blistering, breath-robbing stink. The foggy air seemed to hold something else, too: some tiny particles of black that Sarah brushed hastily from her face.

'The school's on fire!' shouted Alfie. For a moment he and Sarah stared at each other, and then both rushed towards the burning building. Sarah immediately seized the large round knob of the heavy front door and twisted it.

'Mr Elmore must still be inside! The door is unlocked!'

'Wait!' exclaimed Alfie, but he was too late. Sarah had already flung the door open, allowing the air to rush in.

First there was a roar which dulled the sound of drunken laughter from the nearby public house on the corner. Then there was a crash.

The windows of the crazy old house burst out of their rotten frames with a huge explosion of sound. The flames rushed out, licking upwards, and then travelling along the worm-eaten crumbling wood of the building. Alfie turned his head away; the heat was scorching his face and his bare legs.

'Quick!' Alfie seized Sarah by the hand and dragged her away.

'Fire!' he shouted. 'Fire! Help! Fire!'

A moment later, the doors of the Cock & Pye public house opened and dozens of drinkers spilled out on to the pavement.

'Mr Elmore!' screamed Sarah, her face red with heat and twisted with anxiety. 'We must rescue him!'

She moved towards the burning building and then stepped back, defeated by the searing heat.

'What about Tom? What if he's in there?' Jack was now at Alfie's elbow, his face glistening white in the glare of the fire and his eyes large and terrified. Sammy was a few paces away, standing patiently with his hand on Mutsy's collar and his blind eyes turned towards the scorching heat coming from what was once the Ragged School of St Giles.

'Send for the fire engine, someone, please!' Sarah begged the crowd that were gathering around, gazing with fascination at the burning house.

'No insurance plaque, Missy,' shouted one man, slightly less drunk than the others. 'No chance of getting a fire engine if the building hasn't been insured.'

That was true; Alfie knew that. Only the rich could afford insurance. The poor relied on their neighbours and just hoped for the best. 'Let's get some water from the pump,' he shouted.

'Free drink for everyone who helps to put the fire out!' shouted the pub landlord. He disappeared rapidly back into the pub and then reappeared with a boy who was sent running down towards St Martin's Lane.

'The pump is over here,' shouted somebody and everyone surged forward.

It was useless, though. Alfie knew that as soon as they started. The landlord provided a few buckets, some people from the rookeries used their own buckets – not wanting to trust these precious objects to any stranger who might steal them – but most people were just dashing pewter pint pots filled with water against the flames. Soon they abandoned their efforts and queued up for the free gin.

'What about Tom?' Jack's voice trembled as he asked the question again. Alfie pulled himself together.

'Jack, you know that Tom is not in there. He was missing for the whole evening. Why should he go back in there after school was over?'

'He might have been hiding somewhere . . . in a cupboard or something.' Jack's voice broke on a sob and he passed his fist over his eyes.

'Never.' Alfie put all his energy into a tone of scorn. 'Why should he hide in a cupboard? Mr Elmore doesn't keep anyone at the school. They are free to go if they want to. Tom's at home. That's where he is, probably toasting his toes by the fire.'

'Here's the fire brigade,' shouted someone from the back of the crowd and everyone cheered.

The heat from the fire had got hotter and hotter and hotter and the crowd had all moved back. Every head turned towards the large cart drawn by four strong horses preceded by the excited boy from the public house. There were ten men in uniform on top of the cart and a large barrel with a pump and a hose.

'There's a man in there, in that building,' yelled Alfie, but something told him that he was wasting his breath.

'Over here,' shouted the landlord. 'The fire brigade is for my public house. I pay the Sun Insurance Company every year. They're coming to protect *my* property.' He pointed up to the lead plaque with a picture of the sun embossed into the lead and painted a bright yellow.

The men on the cart had already spied the plaque. They whipped their horses and forced a way through the crowd. In a moment the water was sprayed over the front of the public house, the spray drenching the poor rags of the crowd around.

'Turn the hose on the Ragged School,' shouted one man, pointing to the burning building. 'Have some mercy.'

'Please!' cried Sarah, tears rolling down her cheeks. 'The teacher might still be in there.'

The fire brigade men made no answer. They were probably used to turning a deaf ear to such pleas and continued to soak the front of the public house.

And then there was a loud sound, rather like a groan, but a groan from a giant. The flames from the Ragged School blazed higher for a moment, then the whole building began to tilt backwards, and, with an enormous crash, it fell and came to rest in a pile of smoking timbers and clouds of dusty plaster.

'Let's get out of here.' Alfie took the decision suddenly. He grabbed Jack by one arm and Sammy by the other. 'Come on, Sarah, there's nothing can be done now. We'll see you home.'

She followed them. He knew she would. Like himself she had been born into poverty, had to look after herself from an early age, had to see terrible things and live through terrible times. He thought he heard her sob, but when she joined him she was walking steadily and she said nothing until they reached the grand house at Bloomsbury Street.

'I've no key; I'll have to wake up the cook,' she said in a voice that she tried to make normal. 'She's a nice woman. I'll tell her about the school and the fire.'

She went down the steps and Alfie waited until he saw the door opened. Once Sarah had gone in, he touched Jack on the arm and they turned back towards home.

Down Endell Street they went without speaking a word, hurrying past Rats' Castle, a lopsided old building housing men and women who would murder for the price of an evening meal. Then into Buckeridge Street, known to be full of thieves, whose cellars joined up with those of Jones Court, so that a person could dodge the police endlessly in the rabbit warren of passages. Jones Court was inhabited by a hard-working colony, well-known for turning out false coins; and Rose Lane, lined with rotting houses, was famous as a training ground for young pickpockets. Was Tom anywhere here? Alfie found himself wondering. During one of their frequent quarrels, his young cousin had threatened to run away and to join the gang led by Jemima Matthews of Rose Lane, a well-known thief-trainer.

It was a relief to get out of St Giles – a place where there was not a single sewer and where the streets were full of unmentionable filth – into the fresher air of Long Acre and then Bow Street. Whatever happened, thought Alfie, resolutely turning his mind from the idea that Mr Elmore, and even Tom, might be dead . . . whatever happened, survival for the living was his business. The rent for the cellar at Bow Street had to be found every week. He had to keep a roof over the heads of himself, his blind brother and his two cousins. A clever boy who could read and write could go far: Mr Elmore had told him that. Perhaps he could train as a teacher, or get a job as a clerk. He didn't dare to think that could be possible, but he knew that even the most educated man would not get a job if he lived in St Giles. The thing was to look respectable and have as respectable an address to live in as possible. Bow Street wasn't great, but it was better than St Giles. And there would be no need to mention that he just lived in a cellar.

'No light on,' said Jack, his voice hoarse, as they rounded the corner of Bow Street. Although the cellar window was below ground, it had a small yard in front of it and usually the light spilled out on to the pavement above.

'He's fallen asleep and let the fire go out.' Alfie was satisfied that his voice was light and reassuring, but he saw Sammy turn his ear towards him. His blind brother could never be fooled. He read the tones of voices as easily as Mr Elmore read the Bible. Still, the important thing was to keep Jack's hopes up so, as they stumbled down the dark steps to the cellar door, Alfie continued, 'He'll be there, Jack. Where else would he have gone?'

But the door was still locked. And the cellar was cold, dark and empty.

Tom had not come home.

CHAPTER 7

IS TOM ALIVE?

There wasn't much to eat for breakfast next morning – not that it mattered. No one had the appetite for it. Sammy chewed a dry crust of bread and then said thoughtfully, 'Let's get Mutsy to track Tom.'

Jack said nothing. He still had most of his slice of stale bread left. Alfie took a bite of his own slice and chewed resolutely. He would need his strength. Tom had to be found.

'Do you think that Mutsy could do that?' Alfie asked.

Sammy shrugged. 'Why not?' he said. 'You trained him to find me, didn't you?'

This was true and there was a time when that had saved Sammy's life. Even Jack looked up with a spark of interest.

'Let's go, then,' said Alfie. He swallowed the rest of his bread and got to his feet. 'I'll tie a rope to him,' he said. 'That way we can follow him and see where he looks. Here Mutsy, boy, where's Tom? Here, sniff here.' He pushed the dog's nose towards the place where Tom usually slept. 'Where's Tom, then, boy?'

In some strange way, Mutsy seemed to understand what they wanted. He sniffed the tatty cushions which Tom used as a bed and then marched resolutely towards the door.

In a few minutes they were all out on the pavement.

'What now?' asked Jack, looking hopefully at Mutsy.

'We'll start at St Giles, in Streatham Street – that's where we saw him last.' Alfie tried to sound more hopeful than he felt.

But when they arrived at the edge of St Giles, his heart sank. Could the dog smell anything here? The foggy air was filled with the choking smell of burnt timber and smouldering plaster. Puffs of smoke still rose suddenly from parts of the old school building. Even though the sun had not yet risen, Streatham Street was full of people, all gazing at the remains of the fire, some even warming themselves by its heat.

'Where's Tom, then, boy?' asked Alfie again, but Mutsy seemed puzzled, fixing his large, intelligent eyes on Alfie and then looking at Sammy.

Alfie grimaced. They had never used Mutsy to track anyone other than Sammy, he realised. Now the dog thought he was being asked to find the blind boy, not his young cousin.

'We're wasting time,' said Jack impatiently after a while. 'Mutsy don't know what you're talking about. I'm going over there.' He strode towards the ruined school.

'You stay here, Sam, with Mutsy.' Sammy would be quite safe in the midst of the crowd watching the fire. Alfie did not want Jack to go among the burning rubble by himself. Jack, though shy and silent with strangers, was as brave as a lion – too brave, sometimes – and Alfie had no intention of allowing him to risk his life searching through the ruins.

'Tom isn't here, Jack,' he said firmly as he caught up with his cousin.

'I have to be sure,' was all that Jack said. 'I'm going in there.'

The stone floor of the Ragged School was still clearly visible, but very little else was left. The fire had licked around the flagstones before leaping up the half-timbered walls and turning them into smouldering piles of ash.

Before Alfie could stop him, Jack was making his way over the floor, almost as though he expected his brother to be hiding somewhere.

'Don't be stupid, Jack, the fire could flare up again any minute.' Anxiety made Alfie's voice sharp, but Jack, normally so easy-going and obedient to his older cousin, now seemed deaf and he continued to make his way through the smoking heaps. Sighing and uneasy, Alfie followed him.

'This was my classroom.' Jack's voice was low as he stared up around him.

'And that was my classroom up there . . .' Alfie stopped in the middle of his sentence. There was something odd lying at his feet, a yellow shape, a bit bigger than a man's foot. He bent down and picked it up. It was hard, now, but he knew what it was. The tinder-dry old cupboard he had put it in was now just a pile of ash, but the clay he had brought from the brickworks was still there, though now utterly changed. It was no longer soft and slimy; it had been baked as hard as any roof tile.

But not before someone had trodden on it.

Stamped into the clay was the impression of a boot.

And beside it were the remains of a tin can, now crumpled by the heat, but once big enough to have held a few pints of oil.

A vivid picture flashed through Alfie's mind. Someone had come in the front door, stepped into the big wooden cupboard, emptied oil over everything, thrust a flaming torch at the paper, then silently stolen out again, allowing the fire to burn inside its hiding place and then to burst out and engulf the whole building.

But did they know that a perfect impression of their right boot had been baked into the clay?

CHAPTER 8

EVIDENCE

Alfie picked up the piece of clay. He would keep that, he thought. It was too big to slip into his pocket, but he disguised it as best he could by also picking up a fairly unburned chunk of wood. Some of the inhabitants of St Giles were doing the same thing, picking through the remains of the smouldering building to find timber for their fires.

'Cor,' said a voice over his shoulder. Alfie swung around. Albert, the monitor, was standing behind him and prodding at the hard lump with his finger. 'Would you look at that,' he continued. 'It's that clay that you put into the cupboard. Blessed if someone didn't stand on it. Lumme, it's as hard as iron. What do you want it for?'

'Do me for a door stop,' said Alfie casually. 'You haven't seen young Tom, have you? He's been missing since last night.'

He was glad that Jack was not there to see Albert shake his head and look around in a shocked way at the burned building. Alfie wondered if there had been any news of Mr Elmore, but decided to say nothing. His first duty was to find Tom. He felt responsible. He should never have forced the boy to go to the Ragged School.

There had always been a problem between Tom and Alfie. Alfie was the oldest member of the gang, the natural leader, but Tom had never accepted that leadership. He and Jack had been taken in by Alfie's mother, their aunt, on the death of their own mother. When Alfie's mother died of cholera, Tom was left angry and defiant. She had spoilt Tom, Alfie thought, remembering how his mother had fussed over her younger nephew more than any of the other boys, including her own blind son, Sammy. Even after her death, Tom always expected to have his own way and his own privileges.

'Let's go,' Alfie said. 'We're wasting time.' Suddenly

an idea had come to him. He remembered seeing Mary Robinson that night. What if she had kidnapped Tom? He turned away from Jack and edged his way through the burning rubble and back to Sammy.

'Do you think that Mary Robinson could have grabbed Tom and done something to him, killed him or something?' He asked the question quickly, before Jack joined them. Sammy had brains and Alfie relied on him for that.

'Not likely,' said Sammy decisively.

'Why?' Alfie was taken aback.

'Well, why should she?'

'Well, she hates my guts, and she saw him with us last night on the way to school, didn't she?' argued Alfie.

Sammy shrugged. 'And what did she see? She saw Tom arguing with you, cursing you, so why should she think that you would care if anything happened to him? Do you know what I think, Alfie? I think he went off with her of his own accord.'

'What are you talking about?' Jack had just joined them.

'Sammy thinks that Tom might have gone off with Mary Robinson – just because he was in a temper with me.'

'He wouldn't do that.' But Jack's face was suddenly hopeful and Alfie hastened to keep those hopes up.

'I think that old Sam here has got hold of something,' he said. 'There's another thing, too. When I was talking to Mr Elmore, he showed me a big pile of leaflets about Mary Robinson that he had ready to give out at the other markets. Tom could have overheard us, because he was just outside the door when I came out. And Mr Elmore told me later that all the leaflets had disappeared. What if Tom stole them and handed them over to Mary Robinson? She might have given him some money and he went off and found a night's lodging. You can sleep at Tom-all-Alone's place for a penny.'

'Or she might have offered him a job,' said Jack excitedly. He had an optimistic nature. 'A boy like Tom could be useful to run errands for her, or something.'

'What are we waiting for?' asked Alfie. 'Let's go and look at Smithfield market.'

Feeling hopeful, he led the way back to the cellar. There was still no sign of Tom, but that didn't seem to matter now that they had an idea to pursue. Alfie put the piece of baked clay, with its imprint of a boot, carefully into the corner and then turned to Mutsy. 'Smithfield, Mutsy!'

Mutsy wagged his long, furry tail so hard that it was like a piece of rope lashing against Alfie's bare legs. Mutsy loved Smithfield market.

Twenty minutes later they were there. Smithfield was the place where all the meat that was brought in from the countryside was sold. Even the posh shops in Mayfair came there to get their meat. The smell was terrible, but none of the boys noticed it. They were used to smells. Mutsy positively liked them and his nose was twitching vigorously. Alfie took Sammy's arm and let Mutsy go. The dog would be no use until he'd had a chance to catch some of the big fat juicy rats that hid in every crack of the walls around the market, or swarmed under the tarpaulins that covered the carts.

Sure enough, Mutsy made an instant dash at a cart and neatly scooped up a rat from under its wheels. He had a very good technique for dealing with rats. His pounce was lightning quick and his teeth instantly found the back of the rat's neck. After a minute there was nothing left except a long scaly tail.

'Good dog you have there, lads,' said the butcher, pausing in his loading of his cart. 'If there's one thing I hate, it's a rat.'

Mutsy wagged his tail as if he knew he was being praised and carefully checked the rest of the cart, thrusting his wet black nose under the axle and pawing at the ground beneath the wheels.

'You lads are from Bow Street, aren't you?' asked the butcher. 'I recognise the songbird there.' He nodded towards Sammy before continuing. 'Drop into my shop on Drury Lane later on and I'll have a few sausages for you and a bone for the dog. There's four of you, ain't that right?'

'That's right,' said Alfie. 'You haven't seen my other cousin, Tom? Looks like Jack here, but younger.'

'Lots of boys around. Can't say I've taken much notice.' The butcher gave a nod and went back to his job of loading the meat.

Mutsy had eaten three more rats before they reached the north gate into Smithfield market. There was a tremendous din of animal noises, as farmers from the countryside beyond London queued up to get into the market and sell their cows, sheep, pigs and even their baskets of hens and geese to the stallholders.

It was still very early in the morning and many stalls were not yet open. Some stallholders were still walking around, their faces anxious. Alfie's glance sharpened. These must be the ones who had not yet bought their produce from the farmers. And, of course, to do this, they had to have money. Without money, stallholders could not buy the animals, and, unless they bought and then sold at a profit, they would have nothing to live on. There was one woman who had made a fortune out of this need for ready money on the day of a fair.

'We'll follow them. This is where we'll find Mary Robinson.' Alfie spoke directly into Jack's ear. It was too dangerous to say anything aloud. Mary Robinson had plenty of men working for her. One of them might be on the lookout at that very moment. Alfie dragged his cap low down over his face, though he knew that with Mutsy and Sammy beside him, he would be instantly recognised by Mary Robinson herself.

'Here, boy,' he said to Mutsy. Quickly, he tied a long piece of rope to Mutsy's collar. Now was the moment.

'Find Tom,' he said into Mutsy's large hairy ear. 'Go on, boy, find him.'

This got Mutsy excited. He loved finding games. He gave one quick glance at Sammy just to assure himself that he was coming with them, and then began to weave his way through the crowds.

Had Mutsy understood at last?

CHAPTER 9

THE BODY IN THE CART

Mary Robinson did not require any stall, or any sign. Anyone who needed money knew exactly where to find her. Already there were about thirty people, lining up, many of them clutching a piece of paper or a docket to show that they had paid her back promptly the week before. A man walked the line of the queue, carefully scrutinising the pieces of paper and putting those with a docket at the head of the line. Alfie glanced at him briefly. No point in asking him anything. These men were probably paid to keep anything to do with Mary Robinson a secret.

'I hope Tom notices that Mary Robinson's people

can read and probably write, too.'

Jack nodded at Alfie's whispered joke, but his face was very pale, each freckle standing out like smallpox scars on the white skin. His eyes were everywhere, but the friendly butcher was right. This fair was full of boys: boys helping with the animals, boys carrying trestles, boys hammering stalls together, lifting boxes, holding horses; there were as many boys as cows at Smithfield market.

Mutsy was making steady, leisurely progress through the fair. He did not go near the menacing figure of Mary Robinson, dressed in her usual man's overcoat and hat, her stout, heavy boots planted firmly on the wet, stinking filth of the ground. Luckily, she did not look towards the boys – she was too busy shouting at a woman in a torn shawl with three small children clutching at her threadbare gown.

'It's no good. I'm not lending to you again,' she was yelling. 'Yes, I know you paid me back the money last week, but you were sixpence short on the interest. Just you understand this, all of you,' she shouted hoarsely at the waiting crowd. 'I don't lend money for fun, or because I want to do you a kind deed. I lend money at interest and my rate is twelve per cent, per week. I give you eight half-crowns, you give me back nine. And if you think you can get money cheaper than that, then off with you to Threadneedle Street.'

This raised a big laugh. Threadneedle Street was the place where the banks and the moneylenders of the City congregated. It was a place for the rich, not for the poor stallholders, who lived from day to day – hoping every morning that they would manage to make enough money to feed their families.

'Get off with you, you're wasting my time!' yelled Mary Robinson, and the unfortunate woman slunk away. What would she do now, wondered Alfie. There was only one thing left to her and that was to go on the streets and to beg. London was full of beggars; he had known that since he was six years old. Most of them earned very little cash. It did little good to stand at a street corner and whine. Value for money, that's what you had to give the people of London, the people who had the money to spare. He and his gang did all right. They performed tricks, sang songs, held horses, swept crossings so that ladies and gentlemen could cross roads without getting the muck and mire on their shoes and clothes, worked for shopkeepers, scavenged for coal and wood by the riverside, occasionally stole from stalls and bread vans or even from the pockets of the rich ladies and gents that came to Covent Garden Theatre or Drury Lane Theatre. They did all right and it was up to Alfie to look after the gang and keep each member safe, warm and well-fed.

'Twelve per cent per week comes up to six hundred per cent in the year. Banks only charge rich people eight per cent a year.' Alfie had learned that from Mr Elmore, but his cousin didn't seem interested.

'Mutsy looks like he is going somewhere,' said Jack in a low voice.

Alfie said nothing in reply to this. He did not want Jack to get his hopes up too much, but there was a steady, purposeful pull on the rope from Mutsy, now heading towards the gate.

Outside the gate many large carts were parked. It had been a very cold night with freezing fog everywhere and even now the ground under the carts was still frozen and white with hoar frost.

'Find Tom, Mutsy,' repeated Jack, but since Mutsy had left the market things were not looking too hopeful. Alfie kept a tight grip of Sammy's arm and said nothing. He was still not sure whether Mutsy had even understood the command.

And it began to look again as though Mutsy had not understood. He was checking the carts – looking for rats, thought Alfie. Now the dog pulled impatiently against the rope and Alfie came forward and untied it. Let Mutsy catch another few rats and then they would go back and check the cellar again – perhaps Tom had returned – and if not . . .

And if not . . . then what? Alfie's mind ran out of ideas and he stayed there watching Mutsy. The big dog had checked the grass, and then the wheels of a large, handsome wagon, painted blue with the farmer's name on the front board. The horses were probably still in some cosy, straw-filled stable at the Bishop's Finger Inn, because the shafts rested on the ground.

Mutsy ignored these and went around to the back of the wagon. Before Alfie could stop him, he leapt lightly up and thrust his nose under the tarpaulin that covered it.

'Stop it, Mutsy, come back,' yelled Alfie. They would be in bad trouble if a farmer came out and found the dog in his cart.

For once, Mutsy took no notice, though usually he was very obedient to Alfie. His head had now disappeared under the tarpaulin and his shoulders and body soon followed. Only his tail was left out-side and that was wagging with delight.

In despair, Alfie dropped Sammy's arm and swarmed up the side of the wheel.

The tarpaulin was well tied to the sides of the wagon, but he just managed to get his hand in.

And what he felt was soft, stone-cold, and lying as still as any piece of meat.

Frantically Alfie struggled with the string and managed to achieve a gap in the side of the tarpaulin. Hastily he threw it back.

The light was not good. The freezing fog hung in almost solid yellow veils over the whole of London, but there was just enough light to see what was lying there. It was the body of a boy, badly dressed in a ragged pair of trousers, an old waistcoat and a coat too small and too tight with holes here and there.

The boy did not move, but lay there with closed eyes. Above his mouth and nose there was a thin skim of ice.

It was Tom.

CHAPTER 10

THE TARPAULIN BOYS

For a moment, Alfie thought that Tom was dead. He heard Jack gasp from behind and knew that his cousin feared the same.

Mutsy, however, had no doubts. Within a moment, he had licked the ice from Tom's mouth and was now busily washing the rest of the boy's face. His large, warm, hairy body was stretched out over Tom's body. Jack rubbed the stone cold feet and Alfie chafed the icy hands and after a minute, Tom groaned and then started to shiver violently.

'Let's get you out of here.' No doubt the farmer was tucking into a plate of ham and eggs at the

Bishop's Finger Inn but he would soon be out. Quickly, he and Jack dragged out Tom and then Alfie laced up the tarpaulin ties.

'Let's get you over to the chestnut seller's fire.' He hoisted Tom up on to Jack's back, grabbed Sammy's arm and then went quickly through the gate over towards the place where smoke and flames rose up from an iron brazier. Quite a few people were standing in a queue, waiting for the roasted nuts.

'What about a song, Sammy?' Alfie asked.

'*The Catsmeat Man*?' enquired Sammy with a grin. 'Or would they prefer *Don't Eat Tripe on a Friday*.'

Alfie cast a quick, professional glance over the queue for the hot chestnuts. 'Let's have the *The Catsmeat Man* and start it straight away,' he said, noting the well-dressed, prosperous look of those who could leave their stalls so early in the morning. None of them were sellers of cat's meat, he was sure, so they would not take offence. He ushered Sammy to a place near to the fire. The chestnut seller turned to protest, but then stopped as Sammy's high sweet voice rang out.

Sammy was an extraordinarily gifted singer. He had been taught a wide range of songs by their grandfather, who had travelled from Ireland with his fiddle.

'The boy will need some means of earning his living,' the old man used to say, and with Sammy's bright mind and retentive memory, he was always adding to those songs. But it was the quality of his voice that attracted the crowd. He could reach and hold the highest notes effortlessly and was clever enough to vary his songs and keep his audience. *The Catsmeat Man* was making them all chuckle now and keeping everyone in good humour while they were waiting for their roasted chestnuts. When that finished Sammy's voice soared up effortlessly into the sad Irish song, *The Meeting of the Waters*. One or two of the women in the queue wiped a tear from their cheeks, and the pennies and groats pattered into Alfie's cap, placed at Sammy's feet.

Alfie jerked his head at Jack, still patiently holding the frozen body of his brother. It was now quite safe for the other two boys to crouch down before the fire. The chestnut seller, with an appreciative nod towards Sammy, tipped a shovelful of roasted chestnuts towards Alfie and he passed them to Jack. Even if Tom wasn't able to eat anything, the warmth of the chestnuts placed in his half-frozen hand would help.

The queue grew and grew as the stallholders and the shoppers were attracted by the sound of Sammy's voice, now singing *'The harp that once . . .'*

'Give you a hand,' said Alfie, and without waiting for an answer from the chestnut seller, he fetched some more charcoal and carefully placed some more pieces on top of the burning coals and earned himself another nod from the man. Jack, quick and unobtrusive, started to take some more chestnuts from the sack and as the chestnut seller took the money from the buyers, Jack carried on with toasting the next lot of chestnuts. After a few minutes, Tom sat up and held his frozen hands to the flames.

'That your brother?' The man was looking at Tom.

'Cousin,' said Alfie. 'He's been out all night. We've been looking for him everywhere.'

'One of the tarpaulin boys,' grunted the man, efficiently tipping a scoopful of chestnuts into a paper bag and accepting the twopence. 'I hear that a couple of them died last night in this freezing fog.'

'Tarpaulin boys?' questioned Alfie, tipping some ale from a large bottle into a cone-shaped container and thrusting the bottom of it into the glowing charcoal. On a freezing morning like this, the man was selling as much hot ale as chestnuts.

'Yeah, a gent came around and counted them one night. There were seventy boys, all told, sleeping

64

under tarpaulins in carts and in corners of the market. He said it was a disgrace, but what can be done! Here, take a bit of that ale and pour it down his throat. Run away, did he?'

'That's right, had an argument with his dad,' said Alfie, lying with his usual ease. No one knew who Tom's dad was and of course his mother had died many years ago. He had a feeling, though, that the man would be more friendly if he thought they were from a respectable family, and he was right, because he was told to give some ale to Sammy and to take some for himself and Jack. Another shovelful of chestnuts was poured into his hands and he munched some while Sammy sang,

'The sun came through the frosty mist,
Most like a dead-white moon . . .'

'Tell him to sing more of these cold weather songs,' whispered the chestnut seller in Alfie's ear. 'That's what brings the customers. If I do as much business as this in the next hour, I'll stand you all a slap-up meal at the pie stall.'

And so Sammy sang every winter song that he could think of, sprinkling the light-hearted ones with some Christmas carols and ending up singing plaintively in his beautiful voice,

'Good master and good mistress,
While you're sitting by the fire,
Pray think of us poor children
Who are wandering in the mire.'

Several pitying glances were sent at the four ragged boys and their dog, and a couple of bright silver sixpences sparkled against the grimy torn lining of Alfie's cap.

'Here you are, lads.' The chestnut seller handed over another sixpence. 'Off you go now and have a good meal. I'll be here on the same day next week if your brother wants to come and sing a few more songs like that,' he said to Alfie.

'Thinks I'm deaf as well as blind,' said Sammy with a grin once they were out of earshot of the chestnut stall. 'Or else stupid,' he added. There was no bitterness in his voice, but Alfie felt bad for a moment. If only Sammy was not blind, or if they had not been born poor and left as orphans to fend for themselves . . .

'With a voice like that and the brains and musical talent to match it, we'll have you singing in Covent Garden one day,' his grandfather used to say to Sammy. Still, thought Alfie, he sings outside Covent Garden and who knows what might happen. At least they had a roof over their heads and food to put in their mouths most of the time.

'You all right, Tom?' he said aloud. His young cousin was managing to stumble along now, but it was obvious that his feet were still half-frozen. It worried Alfie that they were not red, but still an odd, blotchy shade of white through the dirt and grime. There was a curiously blank look on Tom's face and he said nothing in reply to Alfie's question.

'You all right, Tom?' repeated Jack. He put his arm around his brother's shoulder, giving him a little shake and looking into the vacant eyes.

'Frost got into his brain.' Alfie was sure that he had heard of this sometime.

'What will we do with him?' Jack looked aghast.

'Get some food into him,' said Alfie. Most of the problems of life could be cured by good hot food, was his experience.

'Four mugs of hot ale and five large pieces of pie,' he said in a lordly fashion to the pieman, handing over his precious sixpences. A few ragged boys hanging around looked at him enviously, but Alfie took no notice. His job was to look after his own gang; he couldn't feed the starving hordes of London. He held the steaming ale under Tom's nose until his young cousin's mouth opened. Then he poured some in.

Tom gave a few gulps and then took the mug in his own hand. A little bit of life and understanding seemed to have come back into his eyes. He took another gulp and then looked at Jack.

'Was the other boy dead?' he asked.

CHAPTER 11

THE BOY FROM THE BRICKWORKS

'What boy?' Jack stared at his brother in a bewildered way.

'The boy from the brickworks. He was running away. I met him outside the school. After . . . after . . .'

'After you had given Mary Robinson them leaflets,' said Alfie grimly. The words 'Hope she gave you something for them' were on the tip of his tongue, but he swallowed them. Tom was looking better, Jack was looking hugely relieved and what was done, was done. Alfie was never one to dwell on the past. 'Go on about this boy from the brickworks,' he said.

'He was running away,' repeated Tom. 'He had

been in the workhouse, himself and his mother, and they apprenticed him to the owner of the brickworks on his eighth birthday. He said it was like being a slave. He never got a penny for himself and all the apprentices were just crowded into a shed and had to sleep on some straw and got hardly nothing to eat. He said that he had to get out of London because if the police caught him he would be put in prison.' Tom took a bite of his pie and added, 'It's against the law for an apprentice to run away before his time is up.'

'And he was with you?'

'It was his idea to hide in the wagon. He thought that the farmer might take him on in the morning. God, my feet hurt.'

'That's good,' said Alfie encouragingly. 'That means that they are beginning to thaw out. Come on, Mutsy, let's go and see if that other fellow is still there.'

There was no sign of the farmer when Alfie cautiously approached the wagon. The tarpaulin was still securely tied, just as he had left it. He took a quick look around; there was no one near so he walked all around the wagon, sticking his hand in through the gaps as far as it would reach. He had got to the far side of the wagon when he heard the noise of a breath, quickly sucked in.

'Don't worry,' he said in a low voice, still checking that the farmer wasn't anywhere near. 'I'm Tom's cousin. I've come to get you. Come and have a piece of hot pie.'

The boy's head of tousled curls appeared. He did not seem in such a bad state as Tom, more used to sleeping in frozen conditions if what he told Tom were to be believed.

'What's your name?' asked Alfie, giving him a hand down and then quickly retying the tarpaulin string.

'I'm Charlie. Is your dog friendly?' He didn't wait for the answer. It was obvious that Mutsy was friendly – his tail was wagging so fast that it seemed to stir the veil of fog that hung over everything. The escaped apprentice bent down and put his arms around Mutsy's neck and buried his face in the big dog's comforting fur for a minute before looking up with a grin.

'I like dogs,' he said as he followed Alfie. 'I was born on a farm. My mother worked as a servant for the farmer. She was turned off when the Missus said that she had stolen some food. She hadn't, it wasn't her, but she was sent away with no references so she couldn't get another job. We came to London, but we were starving and sleeping rough and in the end my mother had to go into the workhouse. That was when

I was young and I don't remember it all too well. I remember playing with the dogs on the farm, though.'

'Was your master at the brickworks a Mr Lambert?' asked Alfie, remembering the man who had wanted to buy the school.

Charlie shook his head. 'Nah,' he said. 'Mr Lambert is the rich gent who wants to knock down the whole of St Giles and build some posh houses there. My master is a brickmaker and he works for Mr Lambert on this job. When the houses on Bloomsbury Street are finished he will probably move on.'

Charlie yawned and then began to shiver. Tom put his arm around the boy's shoulders. Alfie looked from one white face to the other and made up his mind.

'You're welcome to doss down with us for a while,' he said. 'Now let's get home and get you two into the warmth. You look like a couple of ghosts.'

'Hide!' said Alfie urgently, looking around the cellar fearfully. Jack had gone out to get some coal from the riverside and Sammy was sitting in the back of St Martin's Church, listening to the choir rehearsing, so he could learn some new Christmas carols. Tom and Charlie had been playing cards and chatting together when Alfie heard the footsteps on the stairs.

'It might be the landlord or the rent collector,' he whispered to Charlie, pushing the boy into a dark corner and pulling the old armchair in front of him. 'He'd try to charge us extra if he thinks you might be staying here.'

It wasn't the rent collector or landlord, though. It was Sarah. She looked very white.

'They've found Mr Elmore's remains,' she burst out as soon as she came in.

Alfie took a moment to swallow the lump in his throat before answering. 'I knew that he must be dead.'

'Are you coming?' Sarah was on the verge of tears.

'Where?' asked Alfie, his voice hoarse.

'They're carrying the body to St Giles Church this evening. It will be moved to the church at Ludgate Hill tomorrow.'

'I'll come,' said Alfie. 'We'll pick up Sammy on our way.'

Sarah's eyes were on Charlie, but Alfie did not offer to explain. He could easily fill her in as they went.

'You'll stay here with Charlie,' he said to Tom, 'and tell Jack where we've gone, won't you?'

Tom nodded. He and Alfie were still awkward with each other, but it would wear off. Alfie had

73

questioned him enough to make sure that yes, it was Mary Robinson outside the school that night, and it was Tom who had stolen the leaflets and given them to the woman (and only got a few pence in return), but all that he knew was that he went one way and she went the other.

Did she return and set fire to the school? wondered Alfie.

Night was beginning to fall by the time they arrived, after picking up Sammy. There was a coffin on a wagon under the lychgate outside the church. It was a very fine coffin, made from shining, exotic wood – 'mahogany' Alfie heard someone say – and it was bound with strips of gold, or perhaps brass. There was no sign of the dead man's father or brother, the rich goldsmiths of Ludgate Hill, but all around there were about fifty mourning children, pupils of the Ragged School, and many women and men, their clothes in tatters, their faces full of sorrow.

'I'd like to sing a hymn for him,' said Sammy quietly. 'Would you ask the vicar, Alfie?'

Alfie cast a quick glance at the self-satisfied face of the vicar of St Giles. This was the man who had appointed the drunken, violent Thomas Orrack to teach the poverty-stricken children of St Giles at the Ragged School, and who now stood amiably chatting with the disgraced teacher. Did Thomas Orrack, wondered Alfie, feel a hatred for the man who had dismissed him? Did he play any part in the tragic fire at the Ragged School at St Giles? And if he did, was the vicar aware of his actions?

'You go ahead, Sammy,' he said softly. 'You don't need permission. Sing out, now.'

Obediently, Sammy opened his mouth and the golden notes, each pure and perfect, streamed out:

'*Glorious things of thee are spoken . . .*'

As Sammy sang, the poor of St Giles sighed and swayed, and knelt on the muddy cobblestones: the Ashkenazi Jews from Germany and Poland placed the ceremonial cap on their heads and the Catholics from Ireland made the sign of the cross on breast and face and a few passed rosary beads between their grimy, work-worn fingers.

By his side, Alfie was conscious that Sarah was sobbing, but he did not turn towards her. His whole attention was fixed on two very well-dressed men who had just dismounted from a carriage and walked towards the crowd. One was a very old, ill-looking man, walking with difficulty and holding on to the arm of the other. Both held a snowy-white handkerchief in front of their nostrils in an effort to block the noisome smells of St Giles, and they were so alike that it was obvious that they were father and son.

Both faces bore a strong resemblance to the man whose charred remains lay within the ornate coffin in front of them. Neither face looked grief-stricken or even appalled, but there was a difference. The old man's face was blank of expression, pinched and blue around the mouth, and the eyes dull and expressionless. But the younger man's eyes were bright and restless, looking here and there around the crowd and at the derelict houses of St Giles.

The service at the lychgate was brief and the vicar of St Giles said a lot about the distinguished visitors from Ludgate Hill, and very little about the man who had given up riches in order to devote his life to the education of the ragged children of St Giles.

Alfie twisted his cap impatiently in his hands and hardly waited until the coffin was taken into the church before exploding to Sarah.

'*A terrible accident!* That were no accident. He was murdered, that's what he was.'

CHAPTER 12

MURDER HUNT

Sarah stopped and looked aghast at Alfie. 'You can't believe that. The building just went on fire.'

'Very convenient, wasn't it?' sneered Alfie. 'Very convenient for people like Mary Robinson and everyone else who wanted to get rid of Mr Elmore.'

'Shh, keep your voice down,' said Sarah as a burly figure brushed past them, cloak pulled up around the face and hat pulled firmly down.

'I suppose you don't care,' said Alfie angrily.

'Of course I care!' Sarah stopped to face him. 'I knew him long before you. Why should you think that I don't care? Thinking that he was . . . Thinking that it wasn't an accident, that's a different matter.'

'Sorry,' muttered Alfie. He felt a bit ashamed of himself. It wasn't fair to take his anger out on Sarah. Looking at her now, he could see how white her face was and how black shadows under her hazel eyes showed that she had slept little the night before. She had had to endure a day's work until she knew Mr Elmore's fate. All the time that she was scrubbing floors, scouring pots and pans, carrying heavy buckets and beating carpets she had probably swung between hope and dread – and then finally to hear the terrible truth!

'Come back and have some supper with us, Sarah,' he said, thinking of her returning alone to the tiny cold, bare bedroom next the scullery of the big house where she worked. 'We're going to have a good supper tonight. Jack is going to call in at the butcher in Drury Lane on his way back from the river. We've been promised some sausages by him and a bone for Mutsy. Mutsy is doing well today; he caught three huge rats under the wheels of the butcher's cart today at Smithfield.'

'What were you doing at Smithfield?' asked Sarah.

Alfie told her the story of Tom and Mary Robinson and about Charlie, the runaway apprentice from the brickworks. He spoke absentmindedly, though, and Sarah read his thoughts.

'Are you thinking that there might be a connection between Mary Robinson and the fire at the Ragged School?' she asked.

'What do you think?'

Sarah thought about it, frowning in concentration. 'It seems a bit far-fetched,' she said dubiously after a minute. 'So what if a few stallholders don't borrow money from her? Does she really make that much from them?'

'Mr Elmore told me that she is supposed to have a fortune invested in gold,' said Alfie. 'He said that he had heard she had fifty thousand pounds in gold. I was wondering today if he had heard that from his brother or his father. They run a gold merchant's business in Ludgate Hill.'

'Funny that Mr Elmore didn't work there,' said Sarah.

'I suppose he didn't take to the business,' said Alfie, but something was running through his mind and when they reached the police station at Bow Street he stopped.

'You go on to the cellar, Sarah. I'm going to have a word with Inspector Denham.'

'I'll come with you,' said Sarah determinedly and Alfie didn't argue.

Inspector Denham was a small man with heavy, bushy eyebrows. He gave Alfie a keen glance.

'What brings you here today, Alfie?'

'Murder.' Alfie's answer was terse. He stared unflinchingly at the man across the desk.

'Yes?' The bushy eyebrows shot up. He eyed Alfie with annoyance.

Alfie faced him resolutely. Inspector Denham didn't look well, he thought, but he still had to say what he came to say. Sarah glanced from one to the other.

'So, who's been murdered? Give us a name.' Inspector Denham coughed for a few minutes, holding a white linen handkerchief before his mouth and then putting it back in his pocket.

'Mr Elmore, the teacher from the Ragged School in St Giles.'

The bushy eyebrows knitted. The powerful man stared at the shabbily dressed boy. 'There was a fire; I heard that. The man was trapped.'

'Murdered.' Alfie still kept the confident note in his voice. Even Sarah, who knew him well, could detect no note of uncertainty.

'Why do you say that?' snapped the inspector.

'Lots wanted rid of him,' said Alfie succinctly.

'Need more evidence than that; plenty of people want to get rid of me, but here I am,' said the inspector with a hint of grin.

'And if you was to be found dead in your office with the place burned around you, I can assure you that I would investigate your death,' said Alfie grandly.

'Well, that's a bargain, then. But I'll need more evidence before I can investigate the death of Mr Elmore, poor man. You tell me what you know and I'll tell you if there is a case. Who are these people who wanted him dead?'

'First of all there was Mary Robinson – the woman who lends money to the costermongers at Covent Garden. Do you know about her?'

The inspector nodded. 'Yes,' he said cautiously. 'That's my patch, I was aware that something was going on.'

'Charging six hundred per cent. That means that for every hundred pounds she lends, she gets back six hundred.' Alfie suddenly felt a pang. Without Mr Elmore he would never have heard of percentages, let alone understand how they worked. 'He was on to her and he was trying to tell all the costermongers in Covent Garden and the stallholders in the other markets about her tricks.'

'Wasting his time.' Inspector Denham sounded dismissive. 'What else can these poor people do? They haven't enough left over by Sunday night to buy their fruit and vegetables on Monday morning. They haven't a hope of doing without the money lender. Admittedly she's a particularly greedy lady, but other money lenders have disappeared from the markets, these days.'

Alfie thought of the box where, penny-by-penny, sixpence-by-sixpence, the week's rent was kept safe before any money could be spent on extra food or luxuries such as second-hand clothes. There were times when he felt sick and tired of the responsibility, but he now resolved that he would try to be a week ahead in the future. He never wanted to have to rely on someone as ruthless as Mary Robinson for their survival.

'And then there was Thomas Orrack, the fellow that used to teach at the school. Mr Elmore insisted that he be sacked for being drunk and violent.'

'That happened almost a month ago. Why do something now and not then?'

'And then there is Joseph Bishop, the body snatcher,' said Alfie.

Inspector Denham's face darkened. 'If you can pin it on . . .' he began and then tightened his lips.

Sarah shivered. She hated the name of Joseph Bishop.

Alfie gave a half-nod. 'Mr Elmore was warning everyone about Joseph Bishop,' he said in neutral tones.

'Came here a couple of times, but we could do nothing.' The inspector sounded apologetic. 'Seemed we could never catch him in the act. He knew too many ways of hiding if there were any policemen around.'

He brooded for a moment. And then his eyes sharpened. He looked from one to the other.

'Whatever you do,' he said emphatically, 'keep away from Joseph Bishop, both of you. No investigating Joseph Bishop; that's an order. I wouldn't like to feel responsible for anything happening to either of you. Now off you go, the two of you. I'll make a few enquiries, I promise you.'

'Get your men to look at the site – there's a burnt-out oil tin there. Mr Elmore didn't use oil. There was nothing but a few tallow candles there in the Ragged School.' Alfie still did not want to mention the clay footprint. He wanted to think about the significance of this. And, of course, if possible, he wanted to be the one to track down the owner of the footprint.

'Useful piece of information,' said Inspector Denham. He took a shilling from his pocket and placed it on the table. 'Here's something towards the rent. You're managing all right, the four of you, are you?'

'We're managing all right,' said Alfie. He gave a slight grimace at the thought that, with Charlie, the gang was probably now five.

CHAPTER 13

A CLUE TO THE MURDERER

'You eat well!' Charlie swallowed his last sausage and sat back. He was terribly thin, thought Alfie as he poked the fire. He would need a lot of feeding up. He looked at the boy dubiously and Charlie looked back at him hopefully.

'I suppose I should be moving along tomorrow morning,' he said.

Alfie grinned. 'Got a good job lined up at the Bank of England?' he enquired and Charlie laughed.

'I'll be all right,' he said brightly. 'I'll find something.'

'You can stay if you like,' said Alfie carelessly. 'We'll find you something to do. Can you do any tricks?'

'I could teach him,' said Tom eagerly. 'We could work up some sort of routine.'

'If you could get me some clay, I could make some marbles and Tom and I could sell them to kids,' said Charlie. 'Some of the fellows at the brickworks used to do that as a sideline – no one would miss the clay.'

'How would we get clay?' asked Alfie. 'And where would we get the shovel to dig it?

'I can tell you an easy way of stealing some if you don't mind going out at night. I daren't go near the place, myself. That foreman would have me clapped in jail as soon as he laid his eyes on me. He kept telling everyone that the last fellow who ran away got two years' hard labour in the prison. We have to get the clay, though, and then we can sell the marbles for a penny a dozen. It's easy money, the fellow at the brickworks told me that.'

Alfie began to feel interested. He had his own reasons for wishing to have some clay. His gaze went thoughtfully to the chunk of hardened clay, still bearing the distinct mark of a boot sole.

'How hot a fire would you need to get something as hard as this?' he asked, reaching over and handing the lump to Charlie.

Charlie turned it over admiringly in his hand.

'This is as hard as you can get it.'

'Could you make it as hot as that in our fire?'

Charlie shook his head. 'No, not a big piece like that, but the fire there would be all right for marbles.'

'That's not what you were thinking, was it, Alfie?' Sarah's sharp eyes were fixed on his face.

'No,' said Alfie. 'I was thinking about the fire at the Ragged School. You see, I put this clay in that crumbling old timber cupboard by the front door. I reckon that someone put a can of oil into the same cupboard, set fire to it and then sneaked back out. The fire would have burned inside the cupboard for a while . . .'

'And the oil would have made it burn very fiercely,' interrupted Sarah. 'Even oil lamps are very hot, much hotter than timber fires.'

'Let me feel it.' Sammy stretched out his hand and Alfie placed the hard lump on his brother's knee, guiding the sensitive fingers so that Sammy could feel all the imprint of the boot.

'Got a good sole on it – you wouldn't slip with all those ridges, would you?'

Sammy was still running his fingers across the piece of clay. 'Not too large a boot, is it?' he added.

'No,' agreed Alfie. 'Bigger than Jack's, though, isn't

it, Jack? And Jack has big feet for his age. So I don't think it was any of the kids going to the cupboard, and Mr Elmore would have said if he had stood on a lump of clay. He'd have had a word with me about leaving it on the floor.'

'Definitely bigger than my boot,' said Jack, neatly cleaning the frying pan by licking the cooled fat from its surface and then putting it down so that Mutsy could finish the job. He placed the remaining string of sausages in a tin box and then sat down beside the others.

'Bears down heavily on the right foot, too, I'd say.' Sammy had not yet finished with the clay. 'See, this side of the heel is worn down. Do you know what I'd guess, Alfie,' he continued. 'I'd say that the person that wore this boot, walks a bit heavily on that side, not exactly a limp, more like bearing down a bit. Got rheumatism, or something in the left leg. Could be that.'

'So we look for someone who favours one leg when he walks?' Alfie nodded to Sarah. 'At least it's something to get started with.'

'Or someone who favours one leg when *she* walks,' said Sammy quietly. 'Didn't you tell me that Mary Robinson wore men's clothes?'

Alfie nodded. 'That's right, and she does wear boots.

Big woman so she probably would have big feet.'

'So she definitely could be a suspect,' said Sarah.

'Suspect for what?' asked Tom.

Jack was also looking puzzled.

'Alfie thinks that Mr Elmore was murdered – that the fire wasn't an accident but was meant to kill him,' said Sarah.

'And we all went home and Mr Elmore went back upstairs to his office with that little tiny window. That was what trapped him,' said Jack sadly.

'We must find out who killed him,' said Sarah. 'Inspector Denham didn't think it was a murder, so now it's up to us. We've done it before with Mr Montgomery's murder, and we can do it again.'

'Inspector Denham was pretty free with his shillings after you solved the last murder. I remember the slap-up meal we had that night.' Jack rubbed his hands at the thought of it.

'There'll be no reward for the death of Mr Elmore,' said Sarah with a sigh. 'He only mattered to the poor people. That father and brother of his didn't look like they cared.'

'So who are the suspects, then?' asked Tom in a businesslike manner, with an eye on Charlie to see whether he was impressed.

'Mary Robinson is my number one suspect,' said Alfie. 'We know that she had a motive for getting rid of Mr Elmore and we know that she was outside the school that night.' From the corner of his eye, he could see Tom blushing in a shamefaced way and Jack looking worried, so he hurried on. 'But we have to think of Thomas Orrack, too – you remember him? The teacher that Mr Elmore dismissed because he was always drunk and on account of him beating little Emily in the alphabet class just because she didn't understand something, poor mite. And then there is Joseph Bishop. Mr Elmore kept going to the police about him. He warned all the kids to keep away from him and more or less said that he suspected him of murder. That's three suspects to be going on with! Any more that you can think of, Sarah?'

'Not really,' said Sarah, 'but I'll keep my ears open when the servants are having their dinner. Everyone was talking about it today and they'll probably still be discussing it tomorrow. Are you going to tell Inspector Denham about the clay print?'

'No point,' said Alfie firmly. 'He's made up his mind that it's an accident. Anyway, it's better if we solve it ourselves. We've got more brains than those fellows in Bow Street.'

'How are you going to do it?' asked Jack.

'What we need,' said Alfie, 'is to get a print from the right boot of all three of the suspects.'

'So you need some clay!' Charlie had a grin on his face. 'And afterwards we can use it for marbles. That's the great thing about clay. Until the moment it's baked, it can be used again and again.'

'So how do I get it?' Alfie squared his shoulders solidly.

'You'll need to wait until after midnight,' said Charlie. 'Until then the work is going on and it starts again at six o'clock in the morning. But between those times it's quiet. Everything is locked up, of course, but there's a loose board in the fence next to Adeline Street and you can get through there.'

'That's what I'll have to do, then,' said Alfie resolutely. 'I'll just take Sarah home now and I'll have a look at the place so that I know what I am doing when I go there after midnight.'

He didn't like the thought of making his way through St Giles after midnight when Joseph Bishop was abroad, engaging in his body-snatching activities, but he owed it to Mr Elmore to do everything possible to catch his murderer, even if it meant placing a piece of clay under Joseph Bishop's right foot.

CHAPTER 14

A SCREAM
IN THE NIGHT

Alfie was too tense to sleep after he returned from seeing Sarah home, so he just sat by the fire until he heard the bells from St Martin's Church sound the hour of midnight.

In a flash, he was on his feet. Moving silently, he picked up the large key from the mantelpiece and pushed it into his pocket and then, by the dim light of the banked-down fire, he searched around for a sack to carry the clay.

There was no moon, but the gaslights still burned as he made his way down Long Acre and a few carriages and cabs still passed down the road, bringing the rich of London back from their night's entertainment at theatres and eating places. Two constables from Bow Street police station strolled along, their eyes watchful and alert. From time to time, one of them shone the blue lantern in his hand into some dark corner. When this happened, the other stood behind him, alert, with a heavy cudgel in his hand.

Monmouth Street was a different matter. No police constables walked there. It was very dark, and the stench of cesspits mingled with the raw sulphuric smell of fog laden with coal smoke. Most of the gas lamps there had been deliberately extinguished; men and women lurked in doorways, hoping that some adventurous toff with good clothes, a fine watch and money in his pockets could be tempted to come down to have a look at the celebrated Seven Dials. Alfie made sure not to look from right to left, but to stare steadily ahead, keeping to one side of the liquid filth that ran down the middle of the road.

Seven Dials, the point where seven streets met, was famous for heavy drinking. A man called Hogarth had even drawn pictures of it. Alfie had seen them in Mr Elmore's office. Tonight it was in its usual state of uproar. With gin selling for a few pence a measure, most of the inhabitants of St Giles were by now roaring drunk. It seemed that nobody was asleep. With a shudder, Alfie saw one woman sitting on the window-sill of an upstairs room, carelessly dangling her baby by one leg. He stood very still underneath, knowing that it was impossible that he could be sure of catching the baby and that he would probably see its brains dashed out on the cobbles before him if she dropped it.

'Give him here, Jenny,' said another woman, leaning out and grasping the baby's arm. Alfie let out his breath and walked on rapidly, his heart thumping hard. He felt sorry now that he had not accepted the offer of Jack's company. He would have done, if he had not had a lurking fear of Joseph Bishop sneaking into the cellar, perhaps knifing Mutsy and bearing off Sammy. Jack was strong as well as immensely brave. Alfie knew that he could trust the safety of the gang to him.

'Not sure that I fancy doing this again,' he muttered to himself as he left Seven Dials, resolving to take plenty of clay and to make this his last midnight journey.

By the time that he reached Bloomsbury, his courage had come back to him and he strolled along in a nonchalant manner, looking at the gleaming windows and well-scrubbed doorsteps of the posh houses and imagining the army of servants, in their attic rooms, who were needed to keep each of these houses in that state of cleanliness.

Alfie reckoned that it must be about half-past midnight by the time that he reached the brickworks. Already half-built houses rose up all around it. The gas lamps worked well here and, despite the fog, it wasn't long before Alfie discovered the gap in the board fence. He looked all around carefully and then noticed a gleam of blue in the distance. A couple of peelers coming his way, he thought, recognising the distinctive lanterns of the police constables. Quickly he made up his mind. If he were to hide, they might discover him and then they would arrest him on suspicion of loitering to commit some theft. Boldly, he marched straight up to them.

'Can you tell me the way to the Cock & Pye public house?' he asked, trying to imitate Charlie's slightly country accent.

'What do you want with the Cock & Pye public house?' asked one of the constables, eyeing him severely.

'Me ma sent me to get me da out of it and send him home,' explained Alfie with an innocent face.

They both laughed at that and pointed the right way, strolling on without a backward glance.

Alfie gave them a few minutes to disappear and then ran back, moving quietly on his bare feet, until he reached the fence. The fog had got worse and it was no longer possible to see the small gap. Alfie moved carefully along it, running his hand against the slats of wood until he came to the missing piece. With a feeling of relief, he slipped inside and tried to remember exactly what Charlie had said.

First you should come to the kiln, then to the saggers – that's the trays with the wet bricks on them. Then you come to the wedged clay – that's the stuff where all the air and the water bubbles has been thumped out. Don't you touch that – anything taken from that will be missed, and someone will get into trouble. But at the end of the yard you'll find the dug-up clay, just out of the hole. Keep away from that hole – it's deep. And keep away from the shed beyond the hole – that's where the apprentices sleep. They always put the shed with the door just near the hole to stop anyone who might get the lock open and sneak out at night. In the morning they put a board across the hole to allow the apprentices out. One fellow who was stiff with the cold staggered a bit and he fell down the hole and broke his neck.

Easier said than done to keep away from that hole, thought Alfie. Charlie had only been at the brickworks during the day, or at night when torches would have burned to allow the work to go on. He stood very still for a while to allow his eyes time to get used to the darkness and the fog.

And then there was a sudden scream. It rang out, piercing through the fog and the murk. Alfie shuddered. There was something uncanny about it. A vague memory flashed into his mind of his grandfather's tales of banshees who shrieked whenever a death was about to occur. This sounded like a banshee, but then to his relief he heard a chorus of angry yells and shouts and he grinned in a slightly shamefaced way. One of the apprentices had had a nightmare and the others were shouting at him.

Still, it had been fortunate for him. Now he knew where he was and he could avoid the lethal hole in the ground. Quickly he moved around the edge of the brickworks, finding, by a piece of good luck, the wet blocks on their saggers, cautiously exploring the rounded lumps of wedged clay and at last, to his great relief, he came to the great mound of rough clay.

Rapidly he stuffed the sack with as much as he could carry, his heart thumping in his chest. He squeezed his way out through the gap in the fence again, hitched the sack over his shoulder and marched along rapidly. Now he felt full of confidence and planned the good story he would make of this in the morning. He might even wake everyone up and they could have a midnight feast and finish the sausages. He looked forward to telling Charlie all about his adventures.

Alfie decided to avoid St Giles – he'd had enough of that, so he struck out confidently down the broader, well-lit streets. He planned to go down Drury Lane, then cut across to Bow Street through Broad Court.

But somehow or other Alfie made a mistake.

By the time he reached Drury Lane he was yawning. The fog was worse and everything looked unfamiliar.

With a prickle of fear, he realised he had made a mistake. The stench hit him first: that terrible smell of decomposing bodies which had not been buried deeply enough. And then he saw the tall, pointed railings, enclosing a small area of ground. And a pair of gates, not closed, but standing slightly ajar.

Alfie had missed the turning for Broad Court. Instead he had gone down Crown Court and now he was outside the burying ground of Drury Lane.

And there was a figure approaching him from the graveyard. A figure carrying a bulging sack.

CHAPTER 15

THE BURYING GROUND

Alfie wanted to run, but somehow he felt the strength go from his legs. He clenched his teeth and willed courage to come back to him. If Joseph Bishop were guilty of the murder of Mr Elmore, he wanted to see him arrested and convicted. He stayed very still, watching the approach of the man. He strained his ears, but the ground was soft, oozing with filth, and no footstep could be heard.

'Out late.' Joseph Bishop had a hoarse, croaking voice, like the noise of a rusty inn sign creaking in the wind. 'What you got in that sack of yours?'

Alfie had not survived in the hard world of the

slums of London without having quick wits and these worked well now.

'Clay,' he said. Rapidly he threw a handful on the ground between himself and the man. Perhaps he would stop and examine the clay.

But Joseph Bishop kept coming. Alfie felt paralysed with fear. This was the man that everyone dreaded. Even the hardened men of St Giles drew aside when he passed them on the street. A collector of dead bodies, a murderer of children: that was Joseph Bishop's reputation. Alfie had been avoiding him for weeks. Now here he was in this dark and desolate place in the middle of the night, face to face with this man.

And there was no one else around.

Why did the police patrol the wide, well-lit streets of Bloomsbury and leave these dark courts unattended?

Now Alfie could just see Joseph Bishop's face by the solitary gas lamp above the gate of the burying ground. It was a strange face, quite square with a broken nose twisted to one side, a toothless mouth, grey spiky eyebrows and the deep scars of smallpox pitting the surface of his filthy skin. He took a step nearer to Alfie. His footstep made no sound – had he trodden on the clay? Alfie dared not look down. The man stared at him. There was something strange about

Joseph Bishop's eyes. They were a very pale grey and they glittered in the white light of the gas lamp. Alfie stared back at him and felt that he was unable to move away from the uncanny power of those eyes.

'Got something to show you,' the rusty voice creaked on. 'Something you'd like to see. Why don't you come in here with me? Come on; you know that you would like to see it.'

'What?' breathed Alfie. The word seemed to be pulled out from the bottom of his chest. He felt one leg move forward, then moved it back. His leg felt very heavy. Almost as though it were not part of him. 'What is it?' he repeated.

'That would be telling, wouldn't it?' There was a sneer in the man's voice. Once again he held out his hand. 'Come on,' he repeated. 'Got something to show you. Something that sparkles. Something gold. You come and help me to dig it out. You'd like to be rich, wouldn't you?'

'Yes,' breathed Alfie.

'Treasure, that's what you can find in these burying places.'

'Treasure,' repeated Alfie. It was a strange feeling to have words come from his mouth, almost as though they were spoken by someone else, almost as though his voice no longer belonged to him.

'And you've got a little blind brother, haven't you? You'd like him to be rich, too, wouldn't you?'

The fog in London could hang around for days, and even weeks, but a strong east wind might suddenly blow in from the river Thames and in minutes the fog would be gone. Something like this was happening now to Alfie's brain. One minute he was standing there almost paralysed, his eyes held by the strange grey eyes of the man in front of him and the next, the old, sharp-witted Alfie was back.

It was the mention of Sammy that had done it, he thought afterwards, but now he was just conscious of being himself again. He glanced around him furtively and then looked into the burying ground. There was no grass there, only the slimy earth – but in one corner some strange substance, almost like silver moss, gleamed in the light of the gas lamp and attracted his attention. The railings there were broken by rust – some lay on the ground, but one was still upright, just held by one thread of corroded metal. The rest of the metal looked all right, though, and it still had a spear-shaped top attached to it. It wasn't a perfect weapon, but it might be enough. Alfie gave it one lightning glance and then turned back to Joseph Bishop.

Somehow he had to distract the man. Just a moment would do it, he thought. He waited until the man came quite close and then, with a sudden movement, he swung the sack from his back and threw it down between them.

'You may as well have a look and see what I've really got inside there,' he said hoarsely.

Joseph Bishop hesitated, just for a second, but it was enough for Alfie. He whirled around and grabbed the spar from the railings. It resisted for a second, causing his heart to beat wildly with terror, and then it broke away. He flourished it in Joseph Bishop's face, aiming deliberately at those strange eyes.

'Get back,' Alfie spat. 'Don't you touch me. Get back, or I swear I'll blind you.'

Joseph Bishop didn't move back, but he did hesitate. His eyes left Alfie's face for a moment. His face turned to one side. With a feeling of triumph, Alfie gave one last flourish with the iron spar, managing to hit the man a sharp blow on the side of the head. The blow should stun him, or at least slow him down as Alfie got away.

An inarticulate cry of rage burst out from Joseph Bishop. Quickly, he bent down, heaved up the sack of clay and lobbed it at Alfie. Alfie ducked and lashed

103

out with his iron weapon. Another thud, this time just to the shoulder, and the man did not cry out. Alfie struggled to regain his balance. For a moment, he feared that he would lose his footing and be at the mercy of a murderer, but then he straightened up.

The next moment there was a clang and the white light from the gas lamp had suddenly disappeared.

But, before it went, Alfie had seen what was in the man's hand.

It was a large and heavy shovel.

Just then he felt the wind whistle past him. The blow had missed him, but the man was so near that Alfie could hear him breathing.

Crash! This time Joseph Bishop managed to hit Alfie's weapon. The impact almost broke the boy's arm. But what was worse; the iron spar shivered to pieces under the weight of the heavy shovel.

Left in Alfie's hand was just one small, rusty piece of metal, no bigger than the leg of a chair.

CHAPTER 16

FLIGHT FROM THE BODY SNATCHER

Alfie didn't hesitate. The dark could work for him as well as for Joseph Bishop. Instantly, he flung the rusty spar, aiming low, hoping to get it tangled within the man's legs, and then he ran. With no light, he stood a good chance of getting away.

It was no good going back into Drury Lane. It was brightly lit, but there had not been a single person around. It would be no good screaming: no one in the houses and rooms above the shops there would take any notice. Once the theatres and the shops closed, the inhabitants retreated to their lairs in the cellars and attics. No, he would keep away from Drury

Lane. So Alfie flew down through the gloom of Crown Court.

As he ran, he heard a muffled yell behind him and a string of muddled swear words. That fellow is mad, he thought. Deep within him was an intense fear, but above that was the feeling that he could survive this.

And Joseph Bishop pounded behind him.

Ahead, Alfie could see a faint glimmer of light. That was Bow Street. The sight gave him courage and renewed his strength.

Suddenly he felt a blow and then a stinging pain in the back of his legs. Joseph Bishop had slung his shovel after him. The sharpened edge had struck the bare calf of his leg, but still he managed to run on, gasping with pain, but cheered by the growing square of light from Bow Street.

But the wound slowed him, and when he reached the end of Crown Court, Alfie could hear that Joseph Bishop was at his heels. With a tremendous effort of will, he rounded the corner without slackening speed and ran down Bow Street.

There was no time to get the key out of his pocket and open the cellar door – Bishop would catch up with him. So, as he passed the cellar windows, a dull gleam coming from the fire inside, Alfie started to yell.

'Mutsy! Jack!' He screamed so loudly that a window went up across the road and someone shouted at him to be quiet.

But that was not the only sound. Dear old Mutsy! Alfie had hardly finished saying his name before the barking began: loud, ferocious barks from the deep chest of a large dog who loved his master. Alfie put his left hand on the edge of the railings and swung himself around, skidded down the steps and hammered on the door.

Jack had it open almost as soon as Alfie took his hand away. He stared at his cousin with wide eyes. 'What's the matter?' he asked.

'It was Joseph Bishop; he was after me,' Alfie said breathlessly. 'Quick, let's get inside.'

But Jack ran to the top of the steps and looked in both directions. 'No sign of him now,' he said.

'Ran off when he heard Mutsy,' said Alfie carelessly, but his heart did not cease to thump until the door was securely shut behind the three of them. He bent down and stroked the dog, glad of a moment to pull himself together and allow his heart to slow down.

'What's up?' asked Sammy, sitting up in his bed.

'Wait until you hear the story,' said Alfie, beginning to feel rather pleased with himself. He reached out a foot and stirred the heap that was Tom. Eventually a tousled head appeared.

'Tom,' began Alfie and then stopped. He had been about to say in his usual, commanding fashion, 'Tom, old son, put some sausages on', but then he changed his mind. Things had to change between himself and Tom. For too long he had been telling Tom things to do, ordering him to do the cooking, giving him tasks that he felt were beneath his own dignity.

'I was just thinking of putting on some sausages,' he amended hastily.

'Did you get the clay?' Charlie rolled over and tossed back his blanket.

'Joseph Bishop has got it at the moment, down outside the burying ground,' said Alfie casually.

'What!' Tom was on his feet, staring at him. Alfie grinned back at him and made a quick motion with his hand to his mouth. Automatically, Tom unhooked the frying pan from the iron bar across the top of the fireplace and took the string of sausages from the tin. Jack took down the pewter mugs from the shelf and fetched the jug of light ale from its position by the draughty window. Alfie settled himself down to tell his story. He was beginning to feel a lot better.

* * *

'And what about my clay?' asked Charlie when Alfie had finished.

'We'll collect that in the morning from outside the burying ground,' said Alfie nonchalantly. He would make very sure to have Mutsy with him, he thought, although Joseph Bishop wasn't often seen in the mornings. He was one of the many in the parish of St Giles that worked by night and slept by day. 'I'm going to have a sleep now and tomorrow we'll take a bit of clay and see if we can get Mary Robinson's footprint,' he finished. 'We have to solve the murder of Mr Elmore; we can't forget about that.'

'Why Mary Robinson's footprint? Don't you think that Joseph Bishop did it?' Jack stared at his cousin in surprise.

'After all, he nearly murdered you,' added Tom. 'Don't you think that he was the one that burned down the school? He seems like the obvious one.'

'What do you think, Sammy?' Alfie felt confused and uncertain. His leg was hurting him. He transferred some water from the bucket into the kettle that hung over the fire and set it to boil. The doctor who had come to see his mother when she was dying of cholera had given him very good advice. *Drink ale if you can and don't even wash in water from the public pump*

109

without boiling it first, was what he'd said. Alfie didn't go in for washing too much, but he did think that the filth from Joseph Bishop's shovel was not a good thing to be in an open wound. He took a piece of cloth from the basket of rags and added it to the water in the kettle; when boiled, it would serve to wash out the muck from the deep cut on his leg.

Sammy took his time to answer. His blind eyes were fixed on the fire. It was strange how often Sammy seemed to be looking into the fire. It was almost as if he had copied that habit from his dead grandfather, who had so often said, 'I can read everyone's fortune in that fire, there.'

'I've got a feeling that Joseph Bishop is not too right in the head,' said Sammy in the end.

Alfie looked at him with interest. 'Why do you say that, Sam?'

'You said it yourself,' grunted Sammy. 'I've just been sitting here and listening to you. You think to yourself – remember what you told us. What did you say? "I think he's mad."'

'I suppose you think that he's not a body snatcher?' snapped Alfie, fishing the rag out of the kettle with the top of his knife. He allowed it to drip for a moment and then squeezed out some more water. It was as hot as he could bear and he had an idea that would be good for cleaning the wound of filth.

Sammy shrugged. 'I wouldn't know about that,' he said. 'I'm just sitting here and listening to what you say. His words sound mad – that's all that I know.'

Alfie mopped out the cut on his leg, leaving a large clean patch all around it. He stared at the blood on the rag. Already he could imagine the yellow pus issuing from the wound, the deadly symptoms of sepsis, the high fever and the lapse into unconsciousness. His father had died of blood poisoning a year before the fever took his mother. Alfie still remembered the unbelievable speed of his father's decline. He tried to dismiss from his mind the memory of his monstrously swollen arm and the ominous red splotches running down from his armpit. But he could not blot out the picture of his father's dead body with the blackened face. He had been carried from the cellar on an old trestle board, and his weeping widow and children had followed him to the burying ground.

Alfie was beginning to feel rather depressed. He seemed to be no nearer to the solution of the mystery. Perhaps he would never solve it. Perhaps he would not be alive to solve it.

CHAPTER 17

BLOOD POISONING

Next morning, Alfie carefully boiled the rag once again and cleaned his wound with the boiled water. It didn't feel too bad, but he knew that the worst, if it was going to happen, would probably not happen for a few days.

In the meantime, however, he had to keep his mind off it. After breakfast, he decided on the plans.

'You and the others stay here,' he said to Jack. 'I'll take Mutsy and go and fetch that clay. We won't be long.' He spoke briskly, trying to conceal his fear and horror at the idea of going back to that burying ground again.

'Why don't you take Jack with you, too?' asked Sammy. 'Me, Tom and Charlie will be all right here.'

'Are you giving the orders around here?' snapped Alfie. It annoyed him that his brother was so easily able to read the fear in his voice, a fear that he hoped to conceal from everyone.

'Just thought it might be a good idea for Jack to have a look at Joseph Bishop's boot print, if there is one. Two heads are better than one.' Sammy was unconcerned by his brother's moods, but Alfie felt a bit ashamed.

'I suppose you're right,' he said after a minute. 'I'll leave Jack, though. He needs a good warm-up before he goes down to that river. It's perishing cold out there. Will you come with me, Tom?'

Tom gave a careless shrug, but he looked pleased.

'Won't be long,' said Alfie. 'Keep the fire going, Jack. We'll set up a marble-making factory here and we have to keep the workers warm.'

There was no one in the narrow lane of Crown Court. It was a dark place where the sun never penetrated and with the fog it almost seemed like night once they had gone a few yards down the alley. No doors opened on to it; it was just a narrow slit between houses until you came to the burying ground beside an old ruined church. Alfie gulped nervously as the stench hit his nose. He glanced down at his leg. It was throbbing painfully. Perhaps he should tie something over it. Perhaps even this smell was enough to infect an open cut like this.

The sack-load of clay still lay on the ground in front of the gates. The other piece of clay, the lump that he had thrown out, was also still there. It was useless, though. Joseph Bishop had trodden on it, but during the fight with Alfie he had walked on it again and again. The whole piece of clay was just a muddle of different marks.

'That's not much help,' groaned Alfie.

'What about inside the gate?' asked Tom. 'We couldn't take anything back, but we could see if he's left a print.'

'We should have brought the hardened piece of clay to compare it with,' said Alfie, feeling annoyed with himself. His mind didn't seem to be working properly.

'Wouldn't do much good – there's nothing there to see,' said Tom, glancing around at the almost liquid mud. He took one step towards the gate and then stepped back again, his face white. A wisp of white vapour was floating about six feet above the surface of the ground and it was coming towards them. Suddenly the air seemed to smell even worse.

'Let's go,' he said, picking up the bag of clay and shouldering it.

'That's just fog,' said Alfie, but he, too, was anxious to get away.

They were about halfway back down the alleyway, when Alfie stopped and looked back. The ghost-like shape had disappeared and things looked more normal.

'Should we have taken the piece of clay from the ground? It would do to make marbles,' he asked.

Tom gave him a surprised look. Alfie didn't often ask his opinion. 'Nah, leave it,' he said. 'It stinks. It'll have picked up the filth that oozes from that ground.'

Alfie glanced down at his leg and said no more. He would be happy never to go near the place again, he thought. But what about Joseph Bishop? Despite Sammy's remarks, they could not rule out the possibility that Joseph Bishop was the murderer of Mr Elmore.

Ten minutes later, they were back in the cellar. Alfie decided to wash his leg again. This time he boiled two pieces of rag and kept one to tie around the wound.

He felt better when the deep, jagged cut was hidden from view. Then Alfie counted the money in the rent box and decided that they could afford to have a day off from the continual efforts to earn money. Jack had already gone off with a sack to get some more coal, but it was probably useless for Sammy to sing in the street, or for Tom to take Mutsy out to do some tricks, as the freezing fog would drive everyone straight into the shops.

In any case everyone seemed enthusiastic about the marble-making. 'They'd be good if we could colour them,' Charlie said. 'One of the blokes at the brickyard got hold of some coloured powder and he mixed that in with the clay. It looked good.'

'What about painting them?' asked Tom.

'No good,' said Alfie. 'Where would we get hold of paint? We can't afford to buy it and we can't steal a tinful. Besides, no one is out painting houses in this fog and ice.'

'I know where I could get you some green,' said Jack, who had just arrived with half a barrowload of coal. 'There's green powder all over that broken old copper pot out in the back yard.'

'Good idea,' said Alfie heartily. The back yard was full of broken pots and pans. The huge old wash pot had been thrown out into the back yard by a washer-woman who lived on the ground floor, just above their heads, and had been there for as long as Alfie could remember. The rain, mist and fog had turned its original copper-gold shade to an elegant green.

So Jack used his knife to scrape as much powder as possible off it into an old tin can. Under Charlie's direction, they mixed the green powder with some water in a bucket, soaked the clay in it and then each took a lump and began to work the air and the water bubbles out with their knuckles. When that was done, they began to form the marbles.

Sammy was enjoying the work, thought Alfie, as he looked at the busy scene. It was not often that his brother could do things that the other boys did, but he seemed more skilful than Tom at manipulating the clay. Charlie had made one marble for him to feel and after the first two, Sammy didn't seem to need to refer to it again, but continued to turn out perfectly rounded marbles. Alfie decided to leave them to the work and carry on with his investigations.

Mary Robinson was striding around the market, speaking sharply to some unfortunate stallholders, reminding them the money was due the following day, lending a pound to some, crossing others off her list, and followed everywhere by a couple of villainous-looking henchmen who continually wrote in small notebooks.

Alfie spent a long time dodging around the fair, waiting for a good opportunity to take Mary Robinson's footprint. He had thought of bringing the baked bootprint, but had decided it was too big and awkward and would only draw attention to himself. He wanted evidence, evidence that would convince Inspector Denham that she was the guilty person. He had to compare the prints and then it would be up to the police to make her produce the boot. Albert, the Ragged School monitor, would testify that a clean, smooth lump of clay had been placed in the cupboard a couple of hours before the fire and that it had been found next morning with a bootprint baked into it.

Alfie had his plans made. An old sack was thrown over his shoulders as if to shelter his ragged jacket from the worst of the weather and inside that sack was a piece of thin wood with an inch-thick piece of clay moulded on top of it. It would take the print and would be easy to pick up and carry away.

At last his opportunity came.

There was a narrow lane between the flower stall

and the apple stall. Alfie noticed the woman in the flower stall look apprehensively towards the tall, bulky figure of Mary Robinson and then take some money from a box under her counter and start to count it.

As quick as a flash, Alfie took the thin piece of board from his sack and set it on the ground, just beside the flower stall's trestle table.

And then he moved away as rapidly as he had come and sauntered around the back of the apple stall.

'Give us an apple, will you?' he appealed to the seller, a fat, glum-looking woman with cheeks as red as her own apples.

'Not on your life,' she said sourly. 'Why don't you get a job and stop trying to cadge things for free.'

'Just one little apple,' pleaded Alfie. He was anxious to stay near there for a moment.

'You can have this one for a farthing.' The woman sorted through the pile of shining apples until she found a small, wizened one with a large patch of rot next to its stalk.

Alfie handed over the farthing. At least now he had a reason to linger and by taking small, infrequent nibbles, he could make the tiny apple last for a long time. He kept his cap well pulled down to hide his face; he had no desire to be seen by Mary Robinson, but he owed it to the memory of Mr Elmore to identify his killer.

Despite his care, the apple had almost disappeared by the time that Mary Robinson made her way towards the nervous flower seller. It was obvious, straight away, that the woman did not have enough money. She was mopping tears with the corner of her shawl as the moneylender bore down upon her. Alfie froze, the tiny apple in his hand and his mouth opened as he peered from behind the back of the apple stall. Would Mary Robinson step on to the clay? By now, he hated her so much that he wanted to trap her, not just to avenge Mr Elmore, but to relieve the unfortunate stallholders of the London markets of her greed.

For a while, it looked as if she would not step on the clay. Her loud, hoarse voice rose up, the stallholder wept, her henchmen wrote in their notebooks with no sign of emotion, other stallholders nearby kept their heads down, averting their eyes, and Mary Robinson stood there, her men's boots planted firmly on the ground.

And then the flower seller, in desperation, snatched a ring off her hand and held it out towards Mary

Robinson. Mary Robinson took a step forward in order to look more closely . . . And placed one heavily booted foot right on top of Alfie's carefully prepared mould.

But what Alfie had not taken into account was that Mary Robinson was a woman who, despite wearing exactly the same outfit of men's clothes and boots every day, was very particular about her dignity. She looked down with annoyance and then took a closer look. There was the piece of wood and there was the piece of clay with the perfect imprint of her boot on top of it.

'Where did this come from?' Her deep, husky voice was suddenly shrill.

'It was that boy over there. I saw him put it down.' The flower seller pointed immediately at Alfie.

'This boy, ma'am?' The apple seller decided to curry favour from Mary Robinson. Before Alfie could escape, she had knocked his cap off and grabbed him by the cluster of curls on the top of his head. Rapidly one of the two henchmen came around the back and grabbed him by the arms.

'Trying to break my leg, weren't you?' Mary Robinson looked at him sourly. Bending down she picked up the clay mould with the perfect imprint of her foot, reversed it and stamped on it, smashing the wood and reducing the clay to a piece of mud.

'You're the varmint that was giving out the leaflets a few days ago!' She peered closely at him and looked around. The market was full of people. He could see her wondering whether to try choking him again and then deciding against it.

'Take him down to Bow Street police station, George,' she said to the man who was holding him. 'Swear out a statement that he tried to break my leg. You're a witness and you are, too.' She swung around and glared at the flower seller, who nodded in a terrified way.

Alfie allowed himself to be dragged along, taking care to give no trouble to George. He had no worries, now. He would be taken to the police station and he had no doubt that he could convince Inspector Denham that he had not intended any harm to Mary Robinson.

'Shut that door,' shouted the duty sergeant when the constable pushed Alfie inside. The fog entered with them and swirled around the gas lamps. Despite the fire the room was icy cold.

'Accused of harassing a lady in the course of her

business,' explained the constable, jerking a thumb at Alfie.

'Put him in a cell,' grunted the sergeant, busily engaged in inserting wads of paper into the ill-fitting window frames.

'Inspector Denham won't be too pleased if you do that without consulting him,' warned Alfie. He was confident that he could explain himself to the inspector.

'He's not here. He's in St Bart's Hospital with pneumonia,' said the sergeant. 'Take him in to Inspector Bagshott, then. He's a troublemaker, this one.'

Alfie's heart sank. Without his ally, what would become of him?

CHAPTER 18

THE NEW INSPECTOR

The man behind the desk looked with disdain at Alfie. Inspector Bagshott was nothing like Inspector Denham. He was an extremely tall, very thin, very upright man with a beak-like nose, a harsh face and cold, grey eyes. His voice was as harsh as his appearance.

'So what were you up to, if you were not trying to lame the poor lady?' he asked aggressively, after the constable had given his report.

Alfie studied him. He kept his face blank as his mind raced through the possibilities. He could say that he didn't mean any harm, that he had just dropped a clay-covered piece of wood by accident. He was unlikely to be believed, though, and what could be his explanation for carrying the object in the first place? In the end, he decided to tell the truth. This inspector didn't look amiable, but he might be open to reason.

'I was doing a job of work for Inspector Denham,' he said eventually. It wasn't exactly true, but it was the best he could think of.

'Rubbish!' Inspector Bagshott made an angry gesture across the table as if he were on the point of punching Alfie in the face.

'It's the truth.' Alfie stared back at him. The man looked aggressive, but not stupid. Perhaps he could make him understand. 'That lady might be a suspect in a murder case.' Alfie tried to make his voice sound as confident as possible.

'Murder case? What murder case? PC 22!' the inspector roared.

The door opened instantly, almost as though the constable had been standing just beside it.

'Have we a murder investigation going on here?' demanded Inspector Bagshott.

'No, sir.' The constable sounded shocked. 'You would have been informed of the matter the minute you arrived, sir, if anything like that was happening.'

'The murder of Mr Elmore, teacher at the Ragged School,' said Alfie, looking directly at the inspector.

'Unfortunate death through fire, sir,' said the constable smartly, sending a glare at Alfie.

'Murder!' contradicted Alfie. 'Inspector Denham took it seriously.' Alfie, who never minded telling a lie in a good cause, arranged his face to look serious and trustworthy. 'There was a footprint baked into some clay at the scene of the crime,' he went on, 'and Inspector Denham asked me to try to match it. Since Mr Elmore had published a leaflet about Mary Robinson ruining the stallholders by charging so much interest, she hated him.'

The inspector opened his mouth and Alfie rushed on. 'And she tried to murder me, to strangle me because I was handing out the leaflets. She got her hands around my throat. Inspector Denham was interested to hear about that.' He wasn't quite sure whether that was true or not, but obviously the friendly inspector wasn't around to contradict it.

The same thought seemed to cross Inspector Bagshott's mind. He leaned across the desk, both fists planted solidly in its centre and his face a couple of inches from Alfie's.

'I'll give you ten seconds to get out of here,' he said, speaking between his teeth with a hissing sound. 'And if you are ever reported to me again, for any reason whatsoever, then you'll see the inside of a cell – and you won't talk your way out of that so easily.'

Alfie did not stay to argue. The constable flung open the door and Alfie found himself running up Bow Street as fast as his sore leg would carry him.

When he opened the door of the cellar, Mutsy came flying up, his tail wagging frantically and then, his nose going to the sore leg, he sniffed at it gently, looking up into Alfie's face. Alfie looked all around. Everyone was there, including Jack. He had bumped the old wooden barrow down the steps and was just unloading some coal.

'What we need now is some bricks or something like that,' said Charlie, surveying the fireplace with a professional eye. 'We can build a sort of bridge with them and light the fire on top of them – make it really hot and then stick the marbles under the fire on this old tin tray.'

There were plenty of marbles already made and Sammy was adding to them rapidly, placing the smooth, pale green spheres with great precision, with one finger marking out the space between them.

'What about me hauling in a bit of a broken iron pot from the yard?' asked Jack. 'We could cover the tray of marbles with it and heap the fire on top. The metal would get very hot – much hotter than bricks. What do you think, Alfie?'

'Should work,' said Alfie in an authoritative way. He hadn't much idea about what heat was needed to bake marbles, but he was not keen on sending Jack out to steal some bricks. Jack wasn't good at that sort of thing and he himself did not feel like any more encounters with the police.

'This tray will soon be full,' said Tom, coming back from the window, where he had been peering up at the few people who were hurrying home through the freezing fog.

Be full quicker if you worked a bit more, thought Alfie, but he said nothing, just busied himself with boiling up the two pieces of rag and thoroughly washing the cut on his leg. Was the blood beginning to turn a little watery, a bit yellow?

Charlie joined Sammy and began to roll out the marbles, working quickly and efficiently, and Tom did his best to equal his speed as Alfie tied the rag over his wound. Perhaps it would feel better tomorrow.

'Need any help with that, Jack?' he asked when his

cousin had arrived back with half an iron cooking pot.

'Just a one-man job,' said Jack. In his neat way, he shovelled the coals aside, took the tray of marbles, put it in the centre of the embers, placed the curved shell of the broken pot on top, piled up the glowing coals on either side until they were slightly higher than the pot and then filled in the centre with more coal. After a few minutes there was a roaring fire going.

'As hot as any furnace,' said Charlie, licking his finger and stretching out his hand towards the heat.

'It's going to use a lot of coal,' said Jack, looking with satisfaction at the fire.

'I'll give you a hand to get some more,' said Alfie as Jack picked up the handles of the barrow. It was an unpleasant task, but he was glad to be doing something to distract his mind from his worries.

The river was invisible behind curtains of thick yellow fog as they made their way down Drury Lane and then bumped the barrow down the Temple Stairs. Some of the coal boats landed there and there were always some spillages as the coal was shovelled from the barges to the waiting carts. The tide was out and the Thames had shrunken back, leaving a line of objects on the high-water mark: dead dogs, poisoned fish, broken baskets, bits of water-soaked timber and a man's suit of clothes. The clothes were sodden and torn, but as the two boys approached a woman rushed past them, seized the garments, wrung them out as well as she could and then placed them in her basket.

'They'll be on sale in Petticoat Lane next week!' said Alfie with a grin at Jack.

'Good lot of coal, here. Dead tide brings every-thing to the shore.' Jack was always strictly practical and kept his mind on the job in hand.

By the time that they arrived back in the Bow Street cellar, Sarah was there, sitting beside Sammy and helping with the marbles. Alfie felt his own sense of loss rush back when he saw how tired and ill she looked.

'Sleep badly, did you?' he asked, sitting beside her and taking a pinch of clay into his hand and watching how his brother rolled it between his palms.

Sarah ignored his question and he realised that she did not want to talk about Mr Elmore's death, but to concentrate on solving the murder. 'How are you getting on?' she asked after waiting for a response for a minute.

'Not too good,' confessed Alfie. 'Mary Robinson did stand on the clay, but she spotted it immediately and got into a flaring temper. She got one of her bull-dogs to take me to the police station. Inspector Denham wasn't there and the fellow that has taken over threatened me with the cells if he hears any more complaints.'

'It's interesting, though, isn't it, that she got into a temper just to see her bootprint on the clay? Almost as though suddenly she remembered putting her boot on to some clay before . . .' Sarah's face was sharp with interest.

'The clay in the cupboard of the school!' Sammy turned his head towards Sarah.

'That's right – she might not have thought any-thing of it at the time, but then when it happened again, it suddenly flashed on her and she wondered if you had done it on purpose. She knew you was involved with Mr Elmore.'

'Tell her about Joseph Bishop, Alfie,' said Tom. 'Wait until you hear this, Sarah!'

So Alfie told her about Joseph Bishop – this was the second time that he had told the story and he made it even better this time, spinning the fight out and adding in details about how the thrown spar had given him an advantage and what he had shouted at Joseph Bishop. Sarah listened carefully and gave a shiver, but nodded her head when Sammy gave his opinion that the man was mad – perhaps too mad to plan burning down a building just to get rid of Mr Elmore.

'I've been thinking about this,' continued Sammy. 'Why didn't Joseph Bishop just attack him on the street, that's what I say? You mark my words, Alfie. When we find who killed Mr Elmore, it won't be Joseph Bishop. I don't even think that it will be a drunk like Thomas Orrack. I think it will be someone respectable, someone who wanted rid of him but didn't want anyone to guess,' said Sammy confidently.

'Someone like Mary Robinson.' Alfie gave his brother a light punch on the arm to show his agreement.

'Or someone else, someone very, very respectable, someone none of us has thought about,' said Sarah, a little sparkle coming into her eyes. 'I've got some news,' she told them. 'I have found out something very, very interesting indeed. The murder might have been committed by a person that none of us was thinking of.'

CHAPTER 19

A NEW SUSPECT

Sarah looked all around her with a smile on her small, thin face. Jack was looking politely interested, Alfie frowning with concentration, trying desperately to guess, Tom trying to look as though he knew the secret, Sammy placidly continuing to roll out the pale green marbles and Charlie, not so interested, walked over to test the temperature of the fire with a wet finger.

'It was the parlour maid who gave me the idea,' Sarah began. 'She's a great gossip. She overhears everything when she's serving at the meals and keeps a straight face when she's doing it, but then she comes out to the kitchen – you should hear her! Sometimes I think I will die laughing as she mimics all their voices, talking in a really posh way, with deep-down voices for the men, and high, squeaky ones for the women.'

Tom and Charlie laughed heartily at this, but Alfie fidgeted. What had been said? Would they ever get to the bottom of this mysterious fire that killed the man who was doing his best for the ragged children of St Giles?

'Well, apparently today at lunch time, they were all talking about the fire at the Ragged School and the Missus said what a shame it was and then her sister, who is very rich, said, "Poor dear Mr Elmore. What a terrible thing for him."'

'And?'

'*And*,' said Sarah dramatically, 'she wasn't talking about *our* Mr Elmore, she was talking about his father. You know, that old man who was at the funeral? Well, this old Mr Elmore is very, very, very rich and he is dying! His heart is very bad. Apparently no one thinks that he can last too long with a heart as bad as this.'

Alfie frowned. He wasn't quite sure what Sarah was getting at. Sammy, however, had a smile on his face, so Alfie said, 'Go on, Sam, you say it.'

'And this very rich man had two sons a few days

ago. Now he has only one.' Sammy smiled quietly to himself.

'And a few days ago, if he had died, all of his money would have gone to our Mr Elmore, the eldest son.' As she said that, Sarah was watching Sammy, who did not hesitate before answering,

'But now it goes to the brother.'

'That's right,' answered Sarah, nodding vigorously. 'Mr Daniel Elmore.'

And then there was a loud knock on the door. It was the sort of knock that was not done with the knuckles of a hand, but with the tip of a heavy stick.

There was only one person who knocked like that. The rent collector.

Alfie cast one desperate glance at the rent box and then went to the door. The man couldn't be going to put the rent up again, could he?

But it wasn't the rent collector. The man who stood on the doorstep pushed past Alfie and strode into the cellar as if he had a right to be there.

In a second he had taken in everything. The huge coal fire, the six youngsters, the slices of bread and cheese before them and the mugs of ale. 'Nice and well-off, aren't you?' he said, but there was some-thing sinister in his voice.

Alfie looked at him steadily. Thomas Orrack was looking better, he thought. Perhaps he had given up on the drink. He certainly did not seem drunk at this moment; in fact, his glance was very keen as he looked at everyone in the small room.

'I saw the girl come down here,' he said with a nod at Sarah. 'You want to be a monitor, don't you, Sarah? Mr Elmore told me that. Well, I'm setting up a new school, two pence a day, or a penny an evening: I'll be holding it in the parish room next to St Giles Church. The vicar has given me permission. He'll be the one in charge of the school. You'll all be welcome. This will take the place of the Ragged School.'

'Except that the Ragged School was free,' said Sarah quietly.

Thomas Orrack laughed.

It was a false laugh, thought Alfie, looking at him with interest. 'Education is worth a few pence,' he said jovially, glancing around at the six children and then staring hard at Charlie.

It was that stare that determined Alfie. He did not want Charlie's presence to be commented on, or to have to explain who the boy was. He would get rid of the disgraced teacher as soon as possible.

'That's good news, Mr Orrack,' he said politely.

'We'll certainly do our best to attend.'

Tom's head snapped up, but Alfie gave him a furious frown from behind Thomas Orrack's back. Politely, he walked towards the door, holding it open for the teacher and even giving a slight bow before he closed the door. Then he walked back and took his place by the fire.

'Well,' he said, looking around at his gang.

'A penny an evening,' said Sarah sharply. 'There were about fifty children at the school every evening. He would soon start making money.'

'And two pence during the day,' said Alfie.

'And, of course, the vicar will be paying him a salary, too,' said Sammy quietly. 'Did you notice how he said that the vicar would be in charge?'

'But is it enough to commit murder for?' asked Sarah.

'What did his boots look like?' asked Sammy.

There was a startled silence.

'Blessed if I know,' said Jack. 'I forgot to look.'

'So did I,' admitted Alfie.

'It's just that I thought he walked a bit to one side,' said Sammy.

Alfie felt furious with himself. Perhaps Thomas Orrack was the man who set fire to the Ragged

School. It could have been revenge – Mr Elmore had got him sacked – or it could have been a way to get Mr Elmore's position for himself. Alfie made an exasperated sound. How could he have forgotten to check the boots? It would have been easy to spill a little water on the floor, get the man to walk on it, then examine it with a candle after Mr Orrack left.

The problem was his leg, he thought. The pain from it stopped him thinking straight. As time wore on it was getting worse and worse. By the light of the fire he took off the rag and examined it carefully.

Now the cut had closed over, but in its place there was a red, throbbing swelling.

And his head ached. And he felt shivery, and slightly weak.

He looked over at Sammy, sitting peacefully by the fire, his sightless face alive with intelligence. What would happen to him if Alfie died of blood poisoning?

CHAPTER 20

INSPECTOR DENHAM

The next morning, Alfie boiled some water again and this time, as well as putting the two rags in it, he held the blade of his knife in the bubbling water for as long as he could bear the heat.

Then, gritting his teeth, he put the sharp edge of the knife against the swollen lump and sliced into it. A flood of yellow pus came out, and then a little blood followed it.

Now the cut looked much better. It was clean and the swelling was less. Alfie began to feel cheerful as he wiped away the fluid and then tied the rag over it again. His head still felt heavy and he was still unusually cold, but he buttoned an old waistcoat of his father's over his jacket and set to work to wash Sammy's hair and get him as tidy as possible.

There were only a few good pieces of clothing in the cellar. Alfie borrowed a scarf from Jack, a pair of breeches without too many holes from Tom and then found a white shirt which he had snatched from a stall in Petticoat Lane and added his own good tartan waistcoat. Carefully he rubbed out any clots of dirt, cobbled a few holes together with a needle and thread, attacked some grease spots with a piece of stale bread and helped Sammy dress in all the finery. By the end of it, his brother looked pretty good, he thought. Alfie had done his best with his own clothes – they didn't look too different – but he reckoned his appearance didn't matter as long as Sammy looked respectable.

'Where are you off to, then?' Jack re-knotted the red scarf around Sammy's neck. It had been kind of him to lend it. It was a good warm scarf and had been given to Jack by a woman whose husband had drowned in the river. Jack had helped to drag the body out and had gone back to the house to console the weeping woman. She had given him the scarf when he went away. He was a nice fellow, Jack;

everyone along the riverside liked him.

'Thought we'd drop into the hospital and see the inspector.' Alfie did not explain any further and was thankful that Jack did not press him.

'Will they let you in?' Tom was very cheerful this morning. They had taken out the tray of marbles from under the coals and found that all, except one or two, had baked hard. The pale green had turned a dark green, and where they had mixed the copper powder with some rust, the marbles were a dark red.

Tom and Charlie practised with them for a while, sending them scooting across the stone floor of the cellar and deliberately crashing them, one against the other. Not one of them was damaged – they were as hard as pebbles. Mutsy watched with interest, his head cocked to one side, and one large ear half-raised in an effort to understand what was going on.

'I'll try, anyway,' said Alfie. 'You and Charlie should go on with the marble-making. You could do with a few hundred before you start selling. We've plenty of clay left. If people buy them, then we can supply them.'

'That looks like St Bart's Hospital, there, Sam, don't it?' Alfie stared thoughtfully at the tall building, carefully spelling out *St Bartholomew's Hospital*.

Sammy laughed quietly. 'I'd be more of a help if my eyes worked better.'

Alfie punched him on the arm and chuckled. There was no doubt that Sammy had a great sense of humour. In some ways, it hurt Alfie when he heard his brother say things like that, but in other ways he was proud of him. He knew that Sammy did not want pity. What he felt about being blind he kept to himself and did not ask for sympathy.

Alfie also kept to himself the feelings of terror and panic that sometimes overwhelmed him when he wondered where the next meal, the next week's rent would come from. He did not want ever to confess that weakness to Sammy or the rest of the gang.

'How's the leg?' asked Sammy.

'Fine,' said Alfie.

'Pity we can't find someone who could give you something for it,' said Sammy.

Alfie did not reply; it was obvious that his brother did not believe him. The bond between the brothers was very strong and both always knew when the other was hurt or worried. But nothing could be done without money to pay a doctor, so there was no point in Alfie talking about his leg. 'Let's go in and visit Inspector Denham,' he said.

St Bart's Hospital was huge. Inside the door was an immense space, the ceiling high above their heads and the tiled floor cool and smooth beneath their bare feet.

'Looks like a church with big high windows and all that,' Alfie whispered in Sammy's ears.

'Bit spooky, like, ain't it?' returned Sammy and Alfie squeezed his brother's arm.

Sammy was right. There was an odd echo from the hurrying footsteps of the doctors and nurses and well-dressed men and women who hurried past, and it did give a weird feel to the place.

At the far end of the hall, there was a woman sitting behind a desk. She looked very forbidding, thought Alfie. He took a deep breath, placed Sammy on a chair by the window, then took one of Mr Elmore's leaflets from his pocket and approached the desk, holding it folded in his hand.

'Message for Inspector Denham from Bow Street police station,' he said curtly.

'Give it here,' the woman said impatiently, holding out her hand.

'Has to be given into his own hand,' said Alfie firmly. 'That's my orders. Inspector Bagshott said

that. These were his very words. *Into his own hands.*'
He stared boldly at the woman and kept the folded leaflet slightly tilted so that she could see the print, but not read it.

After a minute she shrugged her shoulders, consulted a large ledger full of neatly written names in front of her and then said dismissively, 'First floor, room number 222.'

Alfie nodded in an off-hand manner, went back to his brother, grabbed his arm and marched towards the steep stone stairs as quickly as he could before she could change her mind.

By the time that they reached the first floor, Alfie felt as if he could not climb another step. His leg was on fire with pain and he was shivering so much that Sammy noticed. Alfie saw him turn his head with concern on his face as they walked down the corridor. He was in such pain by the time they reached number 222 that he just walked straight in without knocking and immediately sat on a chair, still keeping a tight hold of Sammy's hand. To his relief, only Inspector Denham himself was there in the small room, lying on a high iron bedstead.

'Well, well, what wind brought you two here?' The inspector's voice was weak and hoarse. He was tucked into bed, well-propped up with pillows. He looked pale and he needed a shave.

Alfie wasn't feeling well, but the sight of Inspector Denham wearing a striped nightgown and a nightcap with a tassel, instead of his usual smart, well-brushed uniform, brought a smile to his lips and his courage began to come back.

'Here to investigate your disappearance from Bow Street police station, sir,' he said cheekily. 'Glad to see that you are still with us.'

Inspector Denham gave a grin. He looked more human there in the hospital than he did in the police station.

'Nothing for you to find out. I can tell you the name of what struck me down; it was pneumonia,' he said, his voice a little stronger. 'That's the culprit, but I'm on the road to recovery now. Have some of my hothouse grapes.'

Alfie had never tasted grapes, but he took two, put one in his own mouth and popped the other into Sammy's. It was an astonishing taste, sweet and yet sharp. It made his sore throat feel better.

'You don't look too well yourself,' said Inspector Denham, eyeing Alfie with a sharp glance.

'Just a cut on my leg,' said Alfie. He didn't want the

inspector to think that he was bringing some disease into the hospital.

'So what brings you here, then? Eat the grapes, I don't like them, myself. I'd prefer a whisky but they don't let me have it in here.'

'I've got a bit of evidence for you in the case of the murder of Mr Elmore,' said Alfie.

'Go on.'

He didn't contradict the word 'murder', Alfie noticed. Perhaps Inspector Denham had thought it over and had begun to come round to Alfie's view that the deadly fire was more than a simple accident.

So Alfie told him about the piece of clay, next to the empty oil tin, about Albert the monitor, his witness, and about Mary Robinson's fury when she saw that he had tricked her into leaving an imprint of her foot on another piece of clay.

'I'd swear that she understood what I was doing,' he said.

'Maybe, or maybe not,' said the inspector. 'She's a woman, after all. Women don't like getting dirt on their shoes.'

'She wears boots,' said Alfie dryly. 'Man-sized boots, and the boots looked about the same size as the fire-baked print that I have at home in the cellar.'

'Tell Inspector Denham about Thomas Orrack,' said Sammy.

'You tell him,' said Alfie. A violent fit of shivering had seized him. He had just about been able to say that sentence with his jaw set rigidly to stop his teeth chattering. He swallowed a few more grapes in the hope that they might make him feel better and half-listened to Sammy's account of how Thomas Orrack had opened a fee-paying school in the room by the church of St Giles.

'So you have two suspects.' The inspector sounded thoughtful.

'Three,' said Alfie. 'There's Mr Elmore's younger brother, Mr Daniel Elmore. He will inherit all the money now when the father goes, and the father is in bad health. And then there's Joseph Bishop. He tried to murder me two nights ago. That's how I got this cut on my leg. He hit me with his shovel.'

'Let me see; take off that filthy rag.'

Alfie obeyed. It was true that the rag, which he had boiled clean that morning, was no longer a pale grey, but was covered with the mud and filth of the street.

'Doesn't look too good to me. Just ring that bell there, Alfie, will you?' Inspector Denham sounded more like himself. 'Could you ask one of the doctors to step in here, Nurse,' he said as a starched, uniformed women came bustling in.

A few minutes later, the door opened and a young man, wearing a white coat, came in.

'Ah, Doctor, could you do me a favour and have a look at this boy's leg. He was hit by a shovel that had been used in a burying ground . . .'

Alfie saw the young doctor frown at those words and his heart sank. His guess was right. There was something poisonous about the earth that buried those dead bodies near Drury Lane.

Inspector Denham saw his look and gave him a cheerful wink. 'He's tough. He'll soon be well again,' he said to the doctor.

The doctor already had his hand on Alfie's forehead. 'He's running a fever. I'll take him off and get the leg bandaged up, sir.'

'Just a minute.' Inspector Denham fumbled in the cupboard next to his bed and then produced his purse. 'Here you are,' he said, placing a shilling in Alfie's hand. 'Now you look after your leg and no more investigating. Wait until I'm back at the station and then we can talk about it. Off with you now, go with the doctor. And keep away from that man, Joseph Bishop!'

CHAPTER 21

THE GOLDSMITH AT LUDGATE HILL

'Have you always been blind?' The young doctor had taken several looks at Sammy, touching him lightly on the arm before he spoke.

'Since I was about two or three.' Sammy's voice was placid and he stood very still as the doctor gently pulled down his eyelid and examined his eye by the light of a gas lamp. Alfie looked hopefully at the doctor; he had often wondered whether, if they could pay for medical help, something could be done about Sammy's eyes, but he saw the young man sigh and shake his head.

'Measles, I suppose,' he said quietly. 'The spotted fever, they call it.'

'He's a very good singer,' said Alfie loyally. 'Sing for the doctor, Sammy.'

Sammy broke into a song and the young doctor looked at him sadly, but then clapped enthusiastically.

'What a gift,' he said. 'Well, as they say in church, the Lord giveth and the Lord taketh away. Your sight was taken, but many a person would envy you of that gift to sing.'

Sammy said nothing, but there was a faint flush on his cheeks and a slight smile on his lips.

'Now let's look at this leg of yours, young man,' said the doctor, turning to Alfie.

'I already let lots of the bad stuff out of it with me knife this morning,' said Alfie, watching apprehensively as the doctor took a tray of tiny sharp knives from the shelf.

'More to come, I'd say. First of all, drink this. It will bring your fever down and make you more comfortable. Stop the shivers.' He poured something from a flask into a mug and handed it to Alfie. Alfie swallowed it hastily. It tasted vile, very bitter, but he would have done anything to stop that shivering feeling. That was even worse than the pain in his leg. It made him feel so weak and unwell.

'Now, put your leg up there and try to be brave

because I'm going to hurt you. Would you like to hold your brother's hand?'

'What? Me! Not likely!' scoffed Alfie, trying to raise a laugh and looking uneasily at Sammy. It was a good job that Tom was not there, he thought.

The young doctor spent a long time on Alfie's leg. The smell was terrible; even Sammy's nose twitched from time to time. And the pain was worse. Alfie shut his eyes, clenched his hands, the nails digging into his palms, and concentrated hard on thinking about the fatal fire. Which of the suspects wanted the death of Mr Elmore so badly that they were willing to burn down a building in order to kill him?

'Brave boy,' said the doctor eventually.

Alfie opened his eyes and looked down. Instead of a swollen mass, there was now a large hole in his leg. It looked cleaner, though, and perhaps it might heal now.

'Thank you, sir,' he said.

'Now as soon as you go home, put your leg up on a cushion or something and rest for the remainder of the day. Take some more of the fever drink from this bottle every four hours. You should feel a bit more comfortable by tonight.' He stuffed some paste from a jar into the large hole and then wrapped snowy-white bandages over Alfie's leg.

Alfie looked at it with satisfaction. It was still sore but he had already begun to feel a lot better in himself.

'Wait a minute. Let me see if I can find something to go over that bandage and keep it clean in the streets.' The young doctor went to his black medical bag, rummaged in it and then produced a sock with a large hole in the heel and a smaller hole in the toe. Quickly and efficiently, he sliced the foot off the sock with a couple of slashes from his sharp knife.

'There you are, then,' he said with satisfaction, drawing the sock leg over Alfie's bandage. 'This will keep your leg clean and will save me the trouble of trying to find some kind nurse to darn my stockings.' He gave a quick wink at Alfie and walked to the door with an arm over each boy's shoulder.

'Now remember to rest that leg, or it might swell up again,' he called after them as they went down the corridor.

'Aren't we going home?' Sammy sounded puzzled when they got outside the hospital and turned to the left. Alfie grinned. His brother was as good as Mutsy. He always seemed to know which direction they were heading in.

'You didn't think this smart clobber was just for Inspector Denham, did you? No, we're going to have a little chat with our fourth suspect.'

Alfie shivered slightly. Should he be leading Sammy into this danger? A man who could burn his own brother to death would not hesitate to get rid of two boys. One blind boy and one lame. Did they stand a chance against a murderer?

CHAPTER 22

SAMMY SINGS

Mr Daniel Elmore was not pleased to see them. 'You say my brother wanted you to deliver a message to my father?' While he was speaking, he ran his eyes over both of them. Alfie made sure that his expression was blank and innocent.

The gold merchant's shop was the richest that he had ever seen and the man in front of him, dressed in a frock coat and stylishly fitting trousers, wearing a wonderful gold watch and two or three gold rings on his fingers, was a person that even Inspector Denham would hesitate to annoy.

'That's right, sir.' Alfie's voice was respectful and

humble. 'It was the last thing he said to me on the night when he lost his life in that fire. We're very sorry about your brother, sir, he was very good to all the children in St Giles.' Now he looked at the ground, conscious that Daniel Elmore was scrutinising him and fearful that his own eyes might give away his suspicions of the man.

'Well, tell me and I'll make sure that he gets the message. My father is not a well man.'

'What's this? Stop fussing about me, Daniel. I'm perfectly well, just a little breathless.' The old man came in slowly through a door behind the counter in the goldsmith's shop.

'It's nothing, Father, just a couple of boys trying to beg.'

'I have a message for you, Mr Elmore, from your son that died,' said Alfie hastily. 'From Mr James Elmore.' He spoke fast, fearing that in a moment they would be pushed out of the shop. Already Daniel Elmore had made a signal towards a young shopman at the back of the premises.

'From James?' The old man's face lit up for a brief moment, then fell back into an expression of deep exhaustion.

'Yes, sir.' Alfie seized Sammy by the arm and

dragged him forward. There was nothing for it now but to speak the truth. 'Mr James Elmore wanted you to hear my brother, Sammy, sing. He said that you were an expert, sir.'

The old man smiled sadly. 'James had a lovely voice himself, especially when he was a boy. I wanted to get it trained, but he didn't want to. All his life he wanted to be a teacher.'

'And where did he end up? In that Ragged School!' Daniel Elmore's voice had a sour, jealous note in it.

'Would you listen to my brother sing, sir?' Alfie felt himself trembling with eagerness. He had what he had come for. Daniel Elmore wore polished town shoes, probably with smooth leather soles, not boots with ridged soles, so it was no good getting a print, but he had the right size of feet – quite small for a man. It wasn't just the murder hunt that was on Alfie's mind, though. This would mean so much for Sammy if Mr Elmore's father thought that he had a good voice.

'Come along then, sonny.' The old man smiled at Sammy and stretched out a hand.

'My brother is blind, sir,' said Alfie quickly. Mr Elmore's own sight must be very poor, he thought, if he were unable to see that Sammy was blind at a distance of only a few feet.

'Poor child.' There was a compassionate tone in the voice. No doubt Mr Elmore of the Ragged School had taken after his father. Could Daniel Elmore be so different that he would be ready to murder his own brother?

'Mr Elmore thought his voice was very good and that you would be interested to hear him.' Alfie stopped talking and looked around him in surprise. Mr Elmore's father had led them through a small room, crowded with safes and cabinets and shelves full of cardboard boxes and now they were in a large, bright room with six tall windows stretching from the ceiling almost to the floor, the rich blue silk curtains looped back, showing a garden outside of bright green grass dotted with rounded shrubs, some of them even flowering on this winter's day. It was a beautiful room, full of books, sofas and cushioned gilt chairs, but Alfie's eyes were on a huge piano which stood in the centre.

'What would you like to sing, child?' The old man went straight to the piano and sat on the upright stool.

'I'd like to sing O, *for the wings of a dove*, sir,' said Sammy promptly.

'Mendelssohn!' Mr Elmore looked surprised. 'How did you learn this song, my boy?' he asked gently.

'I learnt it from the choir at St Martin in the Fields church, sir,' explained Sammy. 'I go in and I sit at the back and listen to their songs and I remember them.'

'Like a sparrow picking up crumbs,' mused the old man in thoughtful tones. He sat himself at the huge broad piano and leafed through a pile of sheets until he found the one he wanted. And then he began to play.

Sammy did not sing, or even move. He just sat and listened, his ear turned towards the piano. Alfie was puzzled. Why didn't Sammy sing? Perhaps he wasn't used to singing with music. When he went into St Martin's Church he just listened to the organ and to the voices; he never joined in.

After the last piano note sounded Sammy was very still, but then he sighed. 'I have never heard music like that before,' he said simply. 'You are much better, so much better, than the organist at the church.'

Old Mr Elmore smiled at that. 'I wanted to be a concert pianist when I was your age,' he said, 'but my father had other ideas for me. He wanted me to be a goldsmith and as I was the only son, I had to be a goldsmith and the piano had to take second place.'

He seemed to think for a moment and a great look of sadness came over his face. 'I was kinder to my eldest son, but look what happened to him. . . .'

Alfie thought of saying, 'but he will never be forgotten' but then felt that might be a bit too familiar.

'Now, let's hear you sing, Sammy.' Mr Elmore seemed to put the sad thoughts from him. 'I'll just play the last line as an introduction, then you come in.'

Sammy lifted up his glorious voice and began to sing:

'O, for the wings, for the wings of a dove
Far away, far away would I rove'

The piano followed him, softly and lightly, just a gentle echo.

'In the wilderness build me a nest
And remain there forever at rest —'

Suddenly there was a huge crash, a jangled muddle of notes. Mr Elmore had fallen over the piano and lay there splayed out, his arms stretched in front of him, his lips drawn back from his teeth in a grimace of pain and his eyes wide and staring.

'What's happened? What is it?' cried Sammy.

'Help!' yelled Alfie, running to the door that led into the room behind the shop. 'Help!'

A moment later, he was thrust out of the way by

Daniel Elmore. The shopman followed and then a young boy in a brown linen coat.

'He just collapsed,' stammered Alfie and saw his brother's face grow white. Quickly, he seized Sammy by the arm and moved towards the door. They would be unwelcome here, now; he knew that.

Daniel Elmore was bending over his father, calling his name and shaking him by the arm, but one look at those staring eyes had told Alfie the truth.

The man was dead.

'We'll get out of your way, sir,' he muttered as he steered Sammy through the door into the storage room.

They had just reached the shop when a shout came.

'He's dead!' yelled Daniel Elmore. And then with hardly a second's pause, 'Where are those boys? They tried to rob him; they killed him!'

In a flash, Alfie, dragging Sammy by the hand, was through the door.

There would be no justice for a couple of ragged boys accused of theft and murder. It would be the hangman's noose or a life in prison.

He and his brother had to run for their lives.

CHAPTER 23

STOP, THIEF!

Ludgate Hill was steep and full of people. Alfie thundered along, feeling stabs of pain from his bad leg. He knew that if he were by himself, it would be easier to escape. But it was impossible to leave Sammy and so he had to keep finding openings through the crowds that were large enough for the two boys to go through. He realised, also, that Sammy's blindness made them objects to be remembered.

'Stop, thief!' The cry went up; sooner or later it would happen, he had known that. Now it was impossible to run. Quickly he pulled Sammy into a small deserted alleyway, his eyes searching frantically for some doorway in which to hide until the hue and cry died down.

There didn't seem to be any doorways, though, in this narrow place, so Alfie went on down the alley, keeping in the shadow of the building, holding Sammy by the arm, and feeling thankful that the usual London fog was getting thicker by the minute. He could still hear the shouts of 'Stop, thief' from Ludgate Hill.

And then as his eyes grew accustomed to the dim light, he saw something ahead of him: a wall. His heart sank. Now they would have to turn around and go back. He looked desperately to the left and to the right, but there were no other passages leading off this small alleyway.

'What's wrong?' Sammy knew instantly that there was a problem.

'A wall,' said Alfie. 'Just a wall – no way out of here.'

Sammy said no more; Alfie clenched his teeth. Sore leg or not, he had to see whether there was another alleyway or small court at the back of that wall. It was their only chance. If they went back to Ludgate Hill now they would be immediately spotted – two ragged boys and one of them blind.

'Wait a second, Sam,' he said quietly. 'I'll get up and see if it's possible to get down the other side. If it is, I'll stretch out a hand to you.'

The climb would have been simple for Alfie, had not one leg been sore and stiffly bandaged. Using the muscles in his arms, he eventually managed to lever himself up and reach the top of the wall. Then he got a surprise.

There wasn't another alleyway there, nor a court, nor a small yard heaped with filth: this was a garden with well-cut grass and shrubs dotted around. As he gazed at it, he suddenly remembered the garden outside the windows of the Elmore household; this was it. They must have run in a circle and ended up behind the house.

For a moment he felt panicked, but then he smiled to himself. Everyone had seen the two boys go out of the front door and run down the street beyond. No one would think of looking for them in this garden. And those big round shrubs would make a great hiding place for the next hour.

'I'm reaching my hand down for you now, Sam,' he said in a whisper. 'It's an easy climb, plenty of toe-holds. We'll hide in the Elmores' garden.'

'Can you see into the room?' whispered Sammy when Alfie had settled him behind a sweet-smelling shrub with large white flowers and heavy leathery green leaves.

'Yes, there's no one there,' Alfie whispered back. 'They're all too busy looking for us to bother about the poor man.'

Presently, however, another man was ushered in by Daniel Elmore. Alfie breathed a sigh of relief. It must be a doctor – and the search must have been abandoned. After a few minutes, the dead man was carried through the doorway. No one else came into the room and when Alfie judged that about half an hour had passed, he whispered in Sammy's ear. With cautious glances over his shoulder, he took his brother over to where a large holly bush stood in front of the wall. This would provide good, safe cover, he thought as he began to climb.

The fog was thick by the time they reached Bow Street. Alfie had begun to limp heavily and he was starting to shiver again. Perhaps the fever was coming back, he thought, and then remembered that the doctor had told him to take another drink of the medicine after four hours.

'Gimme a mug, Tom,' he said, sinking down on to the cushion by the fire and taking out the bottle of fever mixture from his pocket and putting an arm around Mutsy. The dog was wild with excitement that the two people he loved the most had come home again.

'Where d'ya get that?' Tom's eyes were on the bottle of medicine.

'St Bart's hospital.' Alfie was too exhausted to explain and Sammy was wrapped in his own thoughts.

Tom wasn't too interested, anyway. 'Look at how many we've made, me and Charlie,' he said, showing a cardboard box heaped up with green and dark red marbles. 'And another lot's baking in the fire.'

'Jack's been getting coal all day,' said Charlie. 'He was half-froze the last time that he came in, but he said he'd do another load. I wanted to help, but he said he was fine.'

Alfie nodded sleepily. Charlie was a nice lad, he thought. It would never occur to Tom to worry about his brother being wet and cold, up to his knees in water in this freezing fog.

'Better have supper ready for him when he comes back,' he said drowsily. He hesitated for a moment and then held out Inspector Denham's shilling to

Tom. 'Get some hot puddings and some ale,' he said, conscious that his voice was weak and strange. He put a hand out and felt Mutsy's warm fur and then blinked. He had to stop his head going muzzy like that. He was the gang leader; he had to organise the selling of the marbles, he had to plan for the winter days.

And he had to solve the mystery of that fatal fire and make sure that the murderer was put behind bars.

By the time Sarah came around after her day's work, the medicine was beginning to work and Alfie was feeling more like himself.

'The Missus had a tea party today and these were left over. The cook told me that I could have them,' said Sarah, putting a brown paper bag on the table and taking out some small chunks of cake.

'Alfie took Sammy to sing for the teacher's father and old Mr Elmore dropped dead when he had a sight of Alfie's ugly face,' said Tom, nudging Charlie to make sure that he got the joke.

'Shut up, Tom,' said Alfie fiercely.

Sarah opened her mouth to say something, then shut it again as Alfie frowned at her. He gave a quick look at Sammy. His brother had been very quiet and pale since they came home. Alfie didn't know what to say to him, but he could guess what Sammy was thinking. For a few minutes there in that room, singing his heart out while the old man had played the piano so beautifully, Sammy had seemed lost in a pleasant dream.

But now the dream had turned to a nightmare. Old Mr Elmore was dead and he and Alfie were being hunted as murderers.

CHAPTER 24

THE SCHOOL IS GUTTED

For most of the next day, Alfie shivered and slept, and shivered and slept. From time to time, Jack brought him something to eat, but he refused it, had some of his fever drink and then slept again. When he woke the following morning, he was conscious of feeling almost too warm. He lay on his cushions for a few minutes, enjoying the feeling. The shivering and the weakness seemed to have gone completely. His leg ached, but that was to be expected. He raised it slightly and inspected it, peeling down the stout, woollen, footless sock. The bandages were still reasonably clean and so firmly put on that Alfie decided that it would be better to leave them alone. There was a slight yellow stain on the outside, but he hoped that was normal.

'Wake up, everyone,' he said cheerfully. 'Work to be done! Let's have a look at them marbles.'

The latest marbles were very good. The rust-coloured ones were particularly hard from the long, hot baking. Alfie described them to Sammy as he put a piece of bread and a mug of small ale into his hands.

'I could make a song about them,' said Sammy thoughtfully. He chewed for a moment, swallowed and then lifted his voice.

'Come, buy our marbles, come buy,
Come, watch them fly, watch them fly,
Green as grass, red as the dawn sky
Come, buy; come, buy; come, buy.'

Sammy's voice soared up in the song, the words that he had just invented blending exquisitely with the tune from a church hymn.

Alfie stared at him thoughtfully and then at Mutsy. His fertile brain was beginning to work on a new act for his gang, something which would draw the attentions of the passers-by at the market. Perhaps they could make up some more words for Sammy's song. Perhaps he could teach Mutsy a new trick, using the marbles.

'Jack,' he said, passing his cousin the jug of ale, 'do

you know of anywhere that you could get a board? About a couple of feet square – something like that.'

'Would it matter if it was a bit rotten?' asked Jack cautiously.

'Not a bit,' said Alfie.

Jack swallowed his bread, washing it down with the ale and got to his feet, closing the door of the cellar behind him.

He was back within a few minutes with a large square piece of board. Alfie gazed at it with satisfaction. 'Got some clay left, Charlie?' he asked casually.

Charlie, looking puzzled, brought the rest of the clay in a bucket.

'Now what you two need to do is to make a sort of track there. Use the clay for walls, make bridges that the marbles can go underneath – something to make a competition.'

Tom looked puzzled, but Charlie got the idea straight away and after a few minutes some miniature roadways and bridges were built.

Alfie turned his attention to Mutsy as Charlie and Tom started practising with shooting the marbles under the bridges. The big dog got up at the click of his master's fingers and came to stand beside him.

'Slowly now,' said Alfie. 'Tom, miss on purpose.

Go on, hit your forehead. Act mad with yourself! Mutsy, hide your eyes!' Quickly Alfie gave a hand signal to Mutsy as soon as Tom crashed the marble against the bridge and Mutsy sat on his hind legs, hid both his eyes with his large hairy paws and gave a groan.

'Good boy, Mutsy,' said Alfie enthusiastically. 'Now, Charlie, you get your marble under a bridge. Cheer when you get it through.'

At the exact second that the marble scooted under the bridge, Charlie's cheer sounded and Alfie said instantly, 'Clap your hands, Mutsy,' quickly giving a hand signal at the same moment. Mutsy sat up on his hind legs and patted his two paws together.

'Good boy!' Everyone was shouting and cheering and Mutsy kept on clapping his paws and then hiding his eyes. Again and again they went through the routine and Mutsy did the right thing every time.

And Sammy sang his song with his unearthly voice, adding more and more verses.

'Should be good,' said Alfie eventually, trying to keep his voice calm. Inside, though, he was quite excited.

'Let's go out and try it now,' said Tom eagerly.

Alfie shook his head. 'Wasting your time today,' he said. 'Keep it until Saturday. That's the day that people bring their children out shopping. You'll make twice as much on Saturday than on any other day of the week. Just keep practising and make some more marbles. Shame to waste a good trick like this through rushing things.'

Alfie waited until Tom and Charlie had settled down to work and then invited Jack to go up to St Giles with him. He felt well this morning and who knows, he thought, they might discover another clue in the ruins of the Ragged School.

The two cousins had expected Streatham Street to be deserted and were surprised, when they rounded the corner, to hear noises of hammering and crashing. The air was full of dust. The old, boarded-up houses opposite the burned-out school were being knocked down. Tall platforms of scaffolding had been built and on top of them men swung sledge hammers, cracking the ancient timbers and sending clouds of dusty plaster sliding to the ground.

'Soon they'll have the whole street cleared,' said Jack, looking around him.

'Might get a job there,' said Alfie, 'but let's just have a quick poke around in the ruins of the school, first. I'd like to see if there was anything that might connect Daniel Elmore to the place, or Thomas

Orrack – or any of them.'

Quickly and unobtrusively, the two boys slipped into the masses of timber and rubble where the Ragged School once stood.

'Wonder if the police took away the oil tin,' said Alfie, looking around. 'No, here it is, still standing there.'

'Can't tell much from an empty oil can,' said Jack, always practical. 'A man is not going to sign his name to it or something. I'll have a bit of root around over here. Good piece of timber there – surprised that no one has took it for firewood.'

Alfie stayed gazing at the tin can; he knew that Jack was right, but still he expected that some clue could be discovered from it. Then he realised that Jack was calling him softly.

'This is why nobody took the chunk of timber!' said Jack when Alfie joined him. 'Look, the letterbox is attached to the other side – be no good to put that on the fire.'

Alfie took the piece of wood and turned it over. The letterbox was there and, what was more, it was almost undamaged. The top had melted a little, but Jack quickly found a narrow, sharp stone and levered it open.

Inside the letter box, singed but still readable, was a piece of paper. Alfie pulled it out. It was one of the printed leaflets. On the one side were the words about Mary Robinson, but on the other side was a drawing – a drawing that was quite like the one that had been handed to Alfie just after Mary Robinson had nearly throttled him.

The drawing was of someone hanging from a gallows. But this time the drawing was carefully done in jet-black ink. And the swinging figure was not a boy, but a man with a heavy beard, dressed in pantaloons and a frock coat.

Under it were letters, printed in rough capitals, by someone who had barely learnt to write and still could not spell.

MSTR LMO

'EL MORE, get it? Mr Elmore!' said Alfie as Jack stared at it in a puzzled way.

So Mary Robinson *had* visited the Ragged School that night.

CHAPTER 25

THE BUILDING SITE

'Any work for two strong boys?' asked Alfie, approaching a man who was shouting orders at the building site.

'The cart's coming, Mr Shawcross, and they haven't finished loading the second one,' shouted a worker from the top of the platform.

Mr Shawcross gave Alfie and Jack a quick up-and-down look and then nodded. 'Two pence an hour to load the carts, half an hour off for dinner. We have two carts and the second one has to be ready when the horse comes back with the empty one.'

'We'd work for two-pence-halfpenny an hour

each,' said Alfie in a businesslike way. 'How many hours?'

'Eight hours, make it three shillings, then, for the two of you. Take it or leave it.'

Alfie shrugged. The pay wasn't great, but it wasn't bad and three shillings at the end of the day would be useful for the rent. And they might find out something useful too.

'We'll take it,' he said.

The work was boring and dirty, loading the broken timber and crumbling plaster on to the carts, with occasional breaks to sprinkle water when the dust of the plaster was choking everyone, but the men were cheerful and friendly.

'You won't know this place in a couple of months,' said one of them to Alfie. 'Mr Lambert will clear the whole of this place and then build some posh new houses here. He's been waiting for ages to do this.'

'What stopped him?' asked Alfie. They had a five-minute break where the men could have a drink of small ale to get the dust out of their throats. Alfie took a swig from the jug, passed it over to Jack, and turned back to the man. He remembered Mr Lambert the property developer from the time he went to get the clay, that terrible evening the school burned down, so he was interested in the news.

'That place over there.' The builder nodded towards the burned-out remains of the Ragged School. 'No point in building posh houses with a place like that across the road. They had to get rid of that, first.'

They had to get rid of that, first. The words echoed in Alfie's mind while he bent and picked up timbers, swung them on to the cart, bent and lifted again and again. Perhaps he had been wrong. Perhaps it hadn't been an act of revenge by Mary Robinson, or Joseph Bishop, or Thomas Orrack. Perhaps it had just been a way for Daniel Elmore to get rid of his brother. Perhaps money was behind it all, not revenge.

Now that the rich goldsmith was dead, Daniel Elmore would not only get his father's wealth, he would also be his brother's heir. The burned-out school building was worth nothing, but, if Mr Lambert would pay any money for the land it had stood on, this piece of Streatham Street would bring Daniel Elmore quite a sum. Now that he had time to think, Alfie began to suspect why Daniel Elmore had been so keen to hand over two ragged boys to the police. He could not have seriously thought that they had anything to do with the death of his father.

'Your leg all right now?' queried Jack.

'Yes, much better,' said Alfie, realising that he hadn't even thought about it for hours. 'Just thinking about something.'

At that moment there was a diversion. The piebald horse that drew the carts was young and mettlesome. From time to time, he seemed to get tired of the monotony – as soon as he arrived back with an empty cart, another full one was harnessed to him. Now he reared up and tried to shake off the cart. The driver, standing by his side, holding the bridle, gave him a vicious cut with his whip and the horse reared up again, his teeth snapping angrily and his hoofs flailing the air until he had knocked the man to the ground.

Jack acted fast. In a second, he had fearlessly leaped to the horse's side and grabbed the reins, hauling the animal to one side before the iron shoes could trample the man on the ground.

'Good boy, good boy,' soothed Jack, stroking the piebald animal and gently scratching behind his ears. 'Easy now, easy,' he whisperered, and the horse turned his head and looked down at the boy almost as though he understood what was being said to him. Quickly Jack jumped on to the cart and shook the reins, saying calmly, 'Move on.' The horse moved a few paces and then stopped on command and Jack climbed down.

'He'll be all right now,' he said and held the bridle while Alfie piled on the last few pieces of timber.

'Why don't you drive him this time?' said Mr Shawcross to Jack. 'It'll give the driver ten minutes' rest; that was a nasty fall. Your mate here can manage on his own until you come back. Not many lads would be as good as you with a horse like that.'

Across the road was a small fat man. Alfie recognised him immediately. It was Mr Lambert – a friendly fellow, he remembered.

But with him was Daniel Elmore.

And they had both turned.

And both had started to walk across the road towards him.

CHAPTER 26

THE
BOOTPRINT

Alfie looked around him in desperation. Where could
he hide? Then he took a deep breath and steadied himself. Now was his chance. He could not worry about
himself. He would never get such a good chance again.

The two gentlemen were obviously coming over to
the demolition site. Mr Shawcross, the foreman, was
greeting them and had already signalled to the men on
the platform to stop work.

Alfie looked around for some place to hide. And
then he stopped. This time Daniel Elmore wore

boots! He had to seize this opportunity. There was no clay around, but the ground was heaped up with crumbling plaster. Rapidly Alfie seized a broom, swept the large pieces of plaster to one side and put them into the cart. But he made sure to leave a good, thick coating of plaster dust on the pathway into the demolition site.

'We're getting on very well, here, sir,' Mr Shawcross was saying. 'We should be finished by the end of the week.'

'I'll have another job for you then.' Mr Lambert was smiling in a satisfied sort of way, his round face creased with good humour and his boot idly tracing patterns in the plaster dust. 'Mr Elmore, Mr Daniel Elmore, is now the owner of the property across the road. We have agreed terms for it, so the site will have to be cleared as soon as possible.'

'What do you think of that, men?' shouted Mr Shawcross cheerfully. 'Another week's work for you all!'

There was a huge cheer at that from the men on top of the scaffolding. Mr Lambert and Mr Elmore looked up, smiling broadly at the men's enthusiasm. While their attention was on the men, Alfie dipped the water container into the water barrel and carefully sprinkled the plaster dust – just enough to dampen it down. Then he quickly took himself off and crouched down behind the waiting cart. He dared not let Daniel Elmore have sight of him. Mr Shawcross wouldn't miss Alfie for a few minutes.

'You might think of investing in some of this property,' Mr Lambert was saying in a low voice as the two men walked down the pathway through the site. 'You can see that we have space here for a good, wide road with blocks of houses on either side.'

Alfie watched them from between the wheels of the cart and was relieved to see that they did not return by the same way, but turned and went along the back of the property.

'Where did you go?' asked Jack when he got back.

Alfie did not answer; he was busy pulling and nudging the cart. The wheels were large and it was almost empty, so it was an easy matter to manoeuvre it above the footsteps in the plaster dust. Plaster dried quickly, he knew that, but it needed protecting in the meantime.

By the time the cart was full and the horse hitched up to it, the boot marks in the plaster had dried. Alfie stared down at them. He had watched carefully. Mr Lambert had walked beside the scaffolding and

Mr Elmore had walked by his side.

But would they match the clay footprint back at the cellar?

'You gave me a fright!' gasped Sarah.

'Thought you'd never come! It's getting late and I want you to look at something.' Alfie sounded impatient. He had been waiting for quite some time outside the railings of the big house in Bloomsbury where Sarah worked. He had a sack in his hand with something heavy at the bottom of it. Sarah looked puzzled, but walked on rapidly. It would do her no good to be seen hanging around on the pavement outside the house with a ragged boy and a large tousled dog.

'I just wanted to make sure that I didn't miss you.' Alfie's voice was apologetic. He understood Sarah's worries. 'I wanted to catch you because the light goes early these days.' He cast a worried look upwards. The fog was coming back again. Soon it would blanket everything and it would be impossible for Sarah to see what he wanted her to see. 'This way,' he said, crossing the road before she could say any more.

Sarah followed him. She knew from the expression on Alfie's face that it was something serious. She was not surprised when he turned to go down Streatham Street. But she was surprised to see what had happened to the street itself.

'They are knocking down all the houses, and they'll be clearing what's left of the Ragged School next week.' Alfie waved his hand around and then stopped. They were too late. The fog had thickened and it was too dark and murky now to see what he needed to show. He bit his lip in annoyance. The plaster was too fragile to lift and it was only a miracle that he had managed to keep the marks intact through the day.

'Wait here, Mutsy, stay with Sarah.' In a moment he was gone, limping down the street, before Sarah could say anything.

The Cock & Pye public house was already doing a good business. Alfie could hear singing and drunken shouts from inside. He approached it cautiously, keeping close to the wall and looking around him continuously. It was an old building, though in better repair than the houses on Streatham Street. There were no gas lamps on this side of St Giles so the Cock & Pye had large pitch torches stuck into iron holders on its outside wall. Alfie sidled up to one of them, then quickly seized the torch and returned to Sarah as fast as he could.

'I had awful trouble keeping this safe all day,' he said as soon as he joined her. He lowered the torch to show a large rotten piece of timber, carefully propped up on a couple of small pieces of wood so that it did not touch the ground. Alfie handed the torch to Sarah and lifted off the timber.

'Footprints,' said Sarah. She looked at him with instant understanding.

Alfie nodded. 'Mr Daniel Elmore, the brother of our Mr Elmore, and the property developer, Mr Lambert, they both walked along here this afternoon. But wait, I have something else to show you.'

He fumbled in the sack and drew out the piece of clay that had come from the cupboard floor in the Ragged School.

It only took Sarah a few seconds of looking from the baked clay to the footprints in the fragile plaster to make up her mind.

'That one,' she said pointing. 'That's the one. It's the exact match. Look at the way the heel is worn down on the outer edge. Do you remember what Sammy said about the villain perhaps leaning more heavily on that side?'

'That's right – he does limp a bit.' Alfie's face was expressionless.

'Mr Daniel Elmore? You didn't tell me that! You didn't say anything about him limping!'

Alfie looked at her. 'That's right,' he said. 'I was just over there,' he continued, pointing to a place just behind where Sarah stood. 'I was hiding under the cart and I watched them walk down there. Mr Lambert walked on that side, just by the scaffolding, and Mr Elmore walked beside him.'

Sarah nodded, moving the torch so that the light shone more clearly on the footprints.

The prints next to the scaffolding showed exactly the same slightly worn heel with the heavy ridges, whorls and nail marks as the baked clay impression from the Ragged School fire.

The second man's print was a smooth leather sole with a perfect heel, showing no sign of wear.

Sarah raised the torch and looked at Alfie's face. He was nodding.

'That's right,' he said. 'It wasn't Mr Daniel Elmore. It was Mr Lambert whose boot made that mark in the cupboard. Mr Lambert was the one who set fire to the Ragged School!'

CHAPTER 27

THE
THREAT

Alfie and Sarah stared at each other across the narrow pathway and then looked down again at the prints. There was no doubt that the print of the man who walked by the scaffolding matched the print from the burned-down school.

'But why?' said Alfie eventually. 'That's what I keep saying to myself. Why murder a man just because he won't sell a house to you? Surely Mr Lambert would think that he might be able to persuade him to do it at some stage. Offer him enough money, offer to build him a new school somewhere else, something like that. Murder seems a bit much.'

'Perhaps he didn't mean to murder him,' said Sarah shrewdly. 'Perhaps he just meant to burn down the school. He waited till all of the kids were well gone – perhaps he never dreamed that Mr Elmore would stay on, preparing his lessons.'

Alfie's mouth tightened. 'He's responsible for Mr Elmore's death all the same and I want to see him behind bars.'

'Can you move those footprints?' asked Sarah. 'We need to have evidence.'

Alfie shook his head. 'I've tried, but they just start to crumble. What will we do? We must do something now – tomorrow may be too late.'

'Go and see the inspector,' suggested Sarah and then bit her lip, remembering the story of Inspector Bagshott and his threat to Alfie. 'No, you can't. He might put you in jail – in any case he will probably not believe you. Let me do it. I owe a lot to Mr Elmore. I'm like you – I want the man who killed him to be punished.'

'No need for you to get involved,' said Alfie gruffly. 'You might get the sack from your job. Anyway, you can't swear to which man made which print – only I can do that.' He frowned. 'Let's go back to Bow Street.'

'Why don't you take Jack with you? Or even let him go on his own?' Sarah made the suggestion just as they turned into Bow Street. She hesitated for a moment, but then said bravely, 'I'm not saying anything against you, Alfie, but some people find you a bit cheeky. Lots of men like Inspector Bagshott would be more ready to listen to someone like Jack who is quiet and shy and very respectful. Jack was there as well as you. He can swear to it.'

Alfie shrugged his shoulders. He felt a bit annoyed, but tried to hide it. 'All right, then,' he said, 'I don't care. I'll take Jack along. He can be a second witness anyway.'

'I'd just send Jack by himself,' said Sarah stubbornly. 'I don't see why not, and then you won't run the risk of being clapped in prison by Inspector Bagshott.'

' . . . so Sarah thinks that you should do the talking.' Alfie was beginning to feel a bit exasperated with Jack. He had explained everything very clearly, had even told him what to say, but Jack just kept saying that he couldn't do it.

'Think of it like an act on the street,' said Alfie with a sudden inspiration. 'Hang on here for a moment, let's just practise. Don't forget to keep calling him "sir". And you can pretend that you were the one that Mr Elmore sent for the clay. And that you were the one that just spotted the footprints in the plaster being the same as the footprint burned into the clay.'

'I'll give it a try,' said Jack in a resigned manner.

'And I'll tell you what, don't ask to see the inspector. Just talk to the constable. Now let's practise all that again.'

'Then I put the wet clay on the floor of the cupboard, sir.' Jack was still very hesitant, but Alfie, listening intently from outside the badly fitting window of the Bow Street police station, felt heartened. Sarah was right. Jack did sound very respectful. When he risked a quick glance into the well-lit room, he could see PC 22 was looking at Jack in a tolerant way.

'And the next morning when we were picking up some pieces of timber for our own fire, I found this.'

Alfie kept crouching down, but he knew that Jack had produced the block of clay, with its clear imprint of a boot.

'Well, that might be useful.' The constable didn't sound too interested. 'I'll talk to the inspector in the morning before I go off duty.'

Alfie breathed a silent prayer of thanks that Inspector Bagshott was not around. Perhaps Jack wouldn't have to see him.

'That's not all, sir.' Jack's voice actually trembled now, but that did no harm.

'Take your time, son, no need to worry.' The constable's voice was kind and soothing.

'I was working at the demolition site opposite today. I was loading the old timbers and plaster into a cart and two men walked across the road and . . . and . . .'

'Go on.' The constable sounded interested now.

'And, sir, the plaster dust was damp and this fellow that owns the property walked on it and . . . and . . .' Jack's words died away. Alfie even heard him gulp noisily before his voice returned to him, 'and he left a print of his boot on the dust . . .' Alfie could not see Jack's face, but he had a horrible feeling that his cousin had forgotten his lines.

'And what?' The constable had a threatening note in his voice.

'It's Mr Lambert!' blurted out Jack. 'He's the one that burned the teacher to death in the Ragged School. My cousin —'

'Get out of here,' shouted the constable. 'Don't you come in here making accusations against a respectable businessman! I'll have you know that Mr Lambert is a personal friend of Inspector Bagshott. Get out immediately, before I change my mind and clap you into a cell.'

Then there was noise of a door opening. Alfie could see Jack's shadow on the pavement. He moved forward and then instantly turned to dart into the shelter of the doorway as another shadow followed.

It was too late, though. He had been seen.

'So that's your cousin, that lying beggar brat, putting you up to tell more lies!' roared the constable. He charged through the door and pounded up the street.

Without Jack, Alfie could not have saved himself. In a moment his cousin was beside him and had gripped his arm, half dragging, half carrying him.

'And you're for the cells, too!' The constable was getting dangerously near when there was a sound of a window being opened.

'Shut your noise,' screamed a voice from overhead. Alfie knew the old woman who lived there. Her temper was bad at the best of times, and now was obviously not the best of times.

Looking over his shoulder, Alfie saw the contents of a chamber pot being emptied from the window. There was a string of curses from the constable and a spatter of something unmentionable on the pavement.

Weak with laughter, Alfie thundered on the cellar door and Jack bolted it shut once Tom had opened it and they were both safely inside.

'That was a lucky escape!' Jack blew out a long breath of relief and then said shamefacedly, 'Sorry, Alfie, I messed it up a bit.'

'Not your fault,' said Alfie. 'Who would have guessed it?' He turned to Sarah. 'Mr Lambert is a great friend of Inspector Bagshott.'

'We'll have to leave it,' said Jack. 'No point in risking our skins again.'

'What do you think, Alfie?' asked Sarah, her eyes on him.

'I'm not giving up,' said Alfie stubbornly. He chewed his lip. If only he could get Inspector Denham out of bed and to the building site first thing in the morning, before anyone started work – but even Alfie realised that was impossible.

It looked as though the man who set fire to the Ragged School was going to go scot free.

CHAPTER 28

THE INSPECTOR ARRIVES

The next morning, Alfie and Jack reached the building site just as dawn was breaking. The fog still hung around and soft black smuts drifted through the air, landing in greasy smudges on their faces and hands. Alfie carried a sack slung over his shoulder holding the baked clay footprint. Once again Alfie compared the two footprints and showed them to Jack.

'Ain't no good me saying they are the same,' said Jack in his practical way. 'Who's going to believe me, or you either, for that matter? Best forget it, Alfie. Hide that sack over there by the scaffolding. They're coming. I can hear the noise of the horse's hoofs.'

'I'll want you to drive the cart today, lad,' said Mr Shawcross to Jack. 'I've sacked the other fellow – no good with a horse, anyway.'

As Alfie watched Jack leave with his first cartload, Mr Lambert, accompanied by Daniel Elmore, arrived in a smart chaise, closely followed by a hackney cab, filled with policemen. Immediately he crouched down beneath the scaffolding.

Inspector Bagshott was first out and he strode up to the foreman.

'Have you got a couple of boys working for you?' he demanded.

'That's right,' said Mr Shawcross. 'One's gone with the cart. The other was here just now. Where's he gone? What's the trouble, anyway?'

'A pair of young criminals, apparently, according to the inspector here.' Mr Lambert seemed quite his usual jolly self.

'And I have a suspicion, from the inspector's description, that one of them might be the boy who caused my poor father's death by trying to rob him,' added Daniel Elmore.

'So we'd be obliged if you would get some of your men to help my constables find the young villains. They can't have gone far if they were here a few minutes ago,' said Inspector Bagshott.

Both men, Daniel Elmore matching his pace to the slightly limping gait of Mr Lambert, walked towards a large pile of broken timber, followed by the inspector, while Mr Shawcross called a few men down from the scaffolding, telling them to help the constables.

Alfie's heart beat rapidly. Almost all of the men, glad of a rest from their hard work, had now joined the constables in the hunt. Sooner or later he would be discovered.

And then there was a neigh and Jack drove the horse and the empty cart on to the building site.

In a second, Alfie was out from under the scaffolding. Clutching the sack, he climbed on to the cart. 'Quick, Jack!' he hissed. 'Get out of here, quick! Up that way!'

'Go on, boy!' shouted Jack.

The lively horse responded instantly to the flick of the reins and the sound of Jack's voice and began to trot. When the animal suddenly realised that, instead of a cartful of heavy timber and plaster, he now just had two skinny boys behind him, the trot lengthened into a gallop and he went thundering up the road.

'Stop them! Stop, thief!' went up the cry. Alfie

looked over his shoulder and saw that Mr Lambert and Daniel Elmore had climbed into the chaise. Moments later, the whip descended on the horse's back and the chaise leapt forward. Alfie looked ahead – the street was fairly empty and they were making good progress – and then he looked back again at the sound of more voices. The three policemen were shouting to a cabman. They were climbing in and the cab set off, rocking violently as it gathered speed.

Streatham Street was full of the clatter of horse hoofs and the roaring of angry voices.

The chase was on.

CHAPTER 29

THE
CHASE

The piebald horse seemed to know that this was a chase. He flew down the street, mane flying, ears back, long legs hardly touching the ground, the almost empty cart rattling behind him.

'Into Broad Street, Jack!' screamed Alfie. Suddenly he knew what he had to do.

Not slacking speed for a moment, Jack swung the horse around into busy Broad Street. Carriages, cabs, road sweepers, dogs, people – all scattered before them. Alfie looked over his shoulder again. The two men, Mr Lambert and Daniel Elmore, seemed to be getting nearer to them, following closely in the traffic gap created by the piebald. The light chaise, drawn by a thoroughbred horse, was gaining on them rapidly. Alfie bit his lip but said nothing. Jack was doing his best. At least the policemen in their hackney cab were far behind them.

'Where next?' gasped Jack.

'High Holborn,' said Alfie. A large bread van, pulled by two horses, turned into Broad Street right in front of the cart. Jack swerved neatly and then pulled the horse to the right.

For a minute, Alfie thought they might have escaped from the chaise, but a glance over his shoulder showed he was mistaken. Mr Lambert was on his feet now, urging his horse as if the streets were a race course.

Suddenly, they slowed down. The traffic was just too dense for Jack to be able to find his way through it. The only consolation was that a heavy brewery cart was still between them and the chaise. Jack was leaning forward, straining his eyes for a gap in the traffic and the piebald, glad to be free of the dreary work of pulling a cartload of rubble, was still as fresh and lively as if it were the beginning of the morning.

Then Alfie saw something that made his heart thud with terror. Mr Lambert had taken a coin from his pocket and was holding it up to the crowd on the pavement.

'A golden guinea for the first man to stop those two boys!' he yelled, pointing right at them.

There was a cart piled high with sacks of coal drawn in close to the pavement.

At Mr Lambert's shout, the coalman immediately dumped the sack of coal and ran straight out into the roadway, his hand outstretched to catch the piebald's bridle. There was no possibility of Jack swerving. He was hemmed in on all sides. The man's hand shot out.

But then the piebald reared up and his neigh rang out like a battle cry. The coalman backed away. The carriage ahead of Jack turned down an alleyway, the piebald bolted as though he saw a winning post ahead of them, and the cart went at a furious pace, hardly slackening for Holborn Hill.

'Turn left, Jack, the next left, into Snow Hill.'

Jack was laughing, but his eyes were locked on the road ahead and his body was tense. Alfie just concentrated. It was important now to make no mistakes, and finding your way in a speeding cart was a different matter to sauntering along the street, looking for road signs.

The next left *was* Snow Hill, and Alfie sucked in a

breath. Not too long now, he thought. The chaise was still on their tail, though, and now the hackney cab was just behind it. Inspector Bagshott was leaning out of the window and yelling, 'Stop, thief!'

There were crowds on both pavements, but no one responded to this cry. The piebald horse was a fearsome sight with froth dripping from his mouth, red nostrils straining, ears flat against his skull and those pounding hoofs striking sparks from the cobblestones.

'Right, Jack, right!' The turn into Cow Lane came almost immediately and Jack almost overshot it, but the piebald horse was game for everything.

'Cross over Giltspur Street and under the archway!' screamed Alfie. There was a shout from a man and a scream from a woman, but Jack was across Giltspur Street almost before the words had left Alfie's mouth.

The archway was built of brick, very tall and the piebald horse clattered under with a noise like thunder.

Across the wide paved area they went until a large doorway was right in front of them.

'Wait here, my man,' said Alfie grandly as he struggled to get down without jarring his swollen leg too much. Over one shoulder was slung the sack with his precious evidence.

'I'll wait around the back so that you won't be noticed,' said Jack in his practical way.

It was too late, though. As the cart moved away, Alfie heard a triumphant shout behind him. The chaise had just emerged from the archway and it was followed by the cab. And they had seen him! The cry of 'Stop, thief!' rose up again and several people stopped to stare.

Alfie struggled up the stairs, knowing that his leg was slowing him up. There was no chance of escaping if he kept on going up in full view of his pursuers, so when he reached the first landing, he limped through the first doorway that he could find. He saw that he was in a large hall full of people, a few white-coated doctors walking quickly, some of the visitors looking at pictures on the wall, some of them standing in groups talking. Every head turned when the boy in ragged clothes came rushing in.

And then every head swivelled again as the door burst open once more and in came three uniformed policemen, closely followed by two angry-faced men.

CHAPTER 30

STOP THAT BOY!

There was no hope of escape. Politely, the crowd stood back, leaving an open pathway for the police to arrest the thief. Alfie looked around desperately. There were people everywhere, all clustering around him and blocking any possible escape. He could not even see a doorway.

Putting his head down, he burst through a crowd of white-coated doctors just as the cry went up: 'Stop that boy!'

But now he was through the doctors and there was a door ahead of him. He was on its other side in a second and had slammed it behind him. There was a long narrow white-tiled corridor there and it was empty of people.

A door on the far side opened and an empty wheeled-chair was thrust out, followed by a young doctor. It was the doctor who had dressed his leg, the doctor who had heard Sammy sing.

Alfie darted across and flopped into the wheeled-chair, clutching the sack on his knee. 'My leg is bad,' he said urgently, just as the door from the big hall was pulled open. He gulped hard and then changed his mind and allowed a sob to break his voice. 'I can't run. Quick, take me to Inspector Denham, room 222! They're trying to get me. Quick!'

The young doctor asked no questions. He took hold of the back of the chair and began to run. Alfie looked back over his shoulder. They had left the crowd behind and reached the end of the corridor. The young doctor turned instantly to the right without slackening his speed.

'Lucky for you that I played ball for Rugby School,' he said as he sprinted to the top of this new corridor and then wheeled sharply to the left. Alfie just had sight of the number 222 before the young doctor had opened the door with one hand and pushed him inside with the other.

'A visitor for you, Inspector Denham,' he said as he closed the door behind them.

Inspector Denham, Alfie saw to his dismay, was not alone. A tall, thin middle-aged woman, dressed in a luxurious velvet coat, was sitting beside his bed.

' . . . this terrible poverty at St Giles —' she was saying as the door was thrown open.

'Alfie!' cried the inspector.

'Sorry to interrupt,' said Alfie feebly. He wondered how long he would have to explain, but he didn't wonder for long.

The door was flung open again and the three policemen crowded into the room, followed by Mr Lambert and Mr Elmore.

Inspector Bagshott immediately grasped Alfie by the arm. 'You young villain,' he said harshly. 'I'll make sure that you get a good long sentence in jail after all of this.' Then he looked at the figure lying on the bed, no longer dressed in gown and nightcap, but wearing a respectable suit, and he gasped.

'What are you doing here, sergeant?' asked Inspector Denham grimly.

'Inspector, sir. Been promoted in your unavoidable absence,' gasped Inspector Bagshott.

Alfie looked from one inspector to the other and

his spirits began to rise. Bullying Bagshott had soft-ened his tone of voice considerably. Alfie decided that the time had come for him to take charge.

'Brought you the bootprint from the Ragged School fire, Inspector Denham,' he said, getting out of the wheeled-chair and advancing towards the bed, holding out the piece of baked clay. The lady sitting beside the bed took it from him firmly, looked at it with curiosity and then passed it over to Inspector Denham. Alfie saw a look of fury on Mr Lambert's face and Inspector Bagshott's cheeks flushed an unpleasant mixture of red and purple.

'This is the boy I was telling you about, from the St Giles area, Miss Burdett-Coutts,' said Inspector Denham and she nodded and turned to Alfie.

'And here,' said Alfie emphatically, 'is the man who made that print.' He pointed dramatically at Mr Lambert. 'His name is Lambert. He made the print on the clay in the cupboard by the door of the Ragged School when he poured the oil all over the paper in the cupboard and set fire to the school. He wanted to get rid of the school so that he could knock down the old houses in the whole street and build some posh new ones.'

'Rubbish,' said Mr Lambert with a scornful laugh.

'This boy is a thief and he caused the death of the father of my friend here.'

'That's true, inspector,' said Daniel Elmore. 'My friend and I have come along with your men to make sure that this boy is taken to court and accused of robbery with violence.'

Inspector Denham weighed the clay in his hands, his keen eyes under the bushy eyebrows studying the clay imprint, then he looked at Mr Lambert.

'Perhaps you would be good enough to take off your right boot, Mr Lambert,' he said softly. 'Hand it to Sergeant Bagshott.'

There was a dead silence in the room. Lambert had been looking at the unwieldy piece of clay on its board with bewilderment, but now Alfie saw his face change. Finally, Lambert had realised the significance of the print.

'I certainly will not take off my boot,' he blustered. 'Why are you listening to a beggar brat who is a liar, a thief and probably a murderer? I'll have you know, inspector, that I have friends in high places and that I will speak to them about you if there is any more of this nonsense.'

'Take off your boot, sir,' repeated Inspector Denham, and he still spoke in that soft voice. 'Constable . . .'

He looked towards the two policemen and, in that instant, Mr Lambert turned and shot through the door, slamming it behind him.

'After him,' roared Inspector Denham. 'Catch him!'

The two constables clutched their hats and started to blow their whistles, but the young doctor was ahead of them. Alfie limped to the door to watch. Inspector Denham got off the bed and stood beside him, and Miss Burdett-Coutts joined them.

Mr Lambert was not a good runner. He could not have outdistanced the constables for long, but the young doctor made sure of the matter by a flying tackle which brought the property developer to the ground. And then he sat on him!

'That's another thing I learned at Rugby School,' he said with a wink at Alfie, who had limped up to him.

'Take off his boot,' ordered Inspector Denham grimly and one of the police constables bent down instantly.

'Get off me!' growled Mr Lambert, kicking out frantically, but the young doctor just grinned and did not move.

'That boot,' said Alfie pointing. He saw Miss Burdett-Coutts look at him with interest and wondered whether she might give him a penny afterwards. There was a bank called Coutts; he remembered that. If she were related to the people who owned that bank, then she must be rich. Rich people – in his experience – rewarded the poor if they interested them, or amused them.

'And . . . they . . . match!' he said, spacing out the words and exaggerating his tone of triumph.

Inspector Denham examined the boot and the imprint carefully and then nodded, raising one bushy eyebrow of enquiry at Mr Lambert.

'Nothing to say?' enquired Inspector Denham.

Mr Lambert had nothing to say, but his face showed fury and frustration. His eyes narrowed as they looked at Alfie, but Alfie did not care about black looks. Neither did Inspector Bagshott, whose eyes were worried as he looked at his superior. Alfie studied his face with inner satisfaction. Inspector Denham looked well and ready for work. No doubt Inspector Bagshott would soon be plain Sergeant Bagshott again, and not in line for promotion either.

'Arrest this man,' said Inspector Denham impatiently.

His colleague said the words reluctantly. 'John Lambert, I arrest you for the crime of starting a fire at the Ragged School of St Giles and being responsible for the death of Mr James Elmore.'

Mr Lambert looked at Sergeant Bagshott with an expression of rage in his face and then across at his friend. 'Why arrest me and not him?' he screamed, pointing to Daniel Elmore.

'I had nothing to do with it!' roared Daniel Elmore indignantly.

'Yes, you did!' shouted Mr Lambert. 'You were the one that had the idea in the first place!'

'I thought you would just set fire to the place over a weekend,' snarled Daniel Elmore. 'I didn't think that you would choose a time when my brother was still in the school. That's what's caused all the trouble!'

From behind the back of the policemen, Alfie grinned at the young doctor and his smile was returned.

The two villains were well and truly unmasked by these words!

CHAPTER 31

CELEBRATION

'Fog again,' groaned Tom, opening the basement window and sticking his head out.

'Should lift,' said Alfie, joining him. 'Smell the air. It's a bit fresher than yesterday.'

Tom was nervous, he knew. This Saturday was going to be the big day. Hundreds and hundreds of marbles were stacked up in a rusty old bucket, ready to be sold. Everything was ready. Sammy and Mutsy had been rehearsed in their roles, the board game had been given the last touches – at Charlie's suggestion a tiny fat clay man, baked hard, was placed beyond the bridges as a target, and on top of the bucket of marbles was a neat pile of small brown paper bags, pinched by Alfie from a stall run by one of Mary Robinson's henchmen.

'Who's going to be in charge?' Tom sounded aggressive, but Alfie did not take offence. He was in a good mood. The murder was solved. Mr Lambert and Daniel Elmore had obligingly incriminated each other. Inspector Denham and Miss Burdett-Coutts had each given him a shilling and the young doctor had dressed his leg again, telling him cheerfully that the wound was much better and that Alfie was obviously born to be hanged!

'You and Charlie are in charge, of course,' said Alfie now. 'Jack and I will just wait around in case you need anything.'

By the time everything was set up the fog had begun to lift, and when the church bells sounded noon, there was quite a crowd around Tom, Charlie, Sammy and Mutsy. Sammy's high, sweet voice penetrated through the noise of the chattering crowds and even rose above the cries of the stallholders. Alfie, from his watching place on a wall, could see heads turning and people moving in that direction.

It helped that the weather was fine and that a few beams of watery sun warmed the dull winter's day. Jack was busy packing the marbles into the bags and taking money. And the cap placed at Sammy's feet was beginning to fill with copper coins; more pennies than halfpennies, or farthings, Alfie noticed with satisfaction when he pushed his way through the crowd and came close to his gang.

Mutsy, of course, was the star. The sight of the big dog clapping his two hairy paws together or hiding his eyes was making all the children shriek with laughter. Alfie noticed that several of the children had a look of envy in their eyes as they watched Tom and Charlie play the game.

'Mister, would you sell that game?' one small boy asked Jack, who looked confused.

'Do you want to have a go?' Alfie moved smoothly forward and applied his toe to Tom's rear to move him out of the way. 'This little gentleman would like to have a turn,' he said suavely, ignoring his cousin's indignant eyes.

That proved a wonderful success. Every child in the crowd wanted to try out the game. It didn't matter whether they managed to knock over the small fat man or not – in fact, it seemed to be even more fun when they missed. Mutsy hiding his eyes was even funnier than Mutsy clapping.

And of course, their parents bought bags of marbles and dropped coins into the cap at Sammy's feet.

'What are we going to have for supper tonight?'

asked Tom as they made their way home. The few rays of sunshine had disappeared and the thick, yellow fog had come down again. The gas lamps were encircled with the hazy mist. Alfie felt his face dampen and knew that it was going to be a bad night. He had sent Jack up to meet Sarah as this was a time when Joseph Bishop might be around. He was glad to see them standing safely by the railings, waiting as the rest of the gang approached.

'Follow me,' he said grandly.

There was a fine public house on the edge of Long Acre. The sign, *The George & Dragon*, was made invisible by the fog, but the windows glowed and the swing door sent out a smell of fine cooking every time someone entered.

Alfie marched resolutely in and his gang followed. The landlord had his back to them when they entered. He was bending down and carefully pulling a huge tray from the oven. Then he straightened and turned around.

On top of the tray was a pie – the largest pie that could be imagined. It was the size of the wheel on Jack's barrow and its crust was golden brown, scattered with ornamental leaves and rosebuds, all made from pastry.

There were several small holes in the crust and from these rose a delicious smell.

Alfie's mouth watered. He knew what was beneath that pastry crust. He had often stood outside the window of *The George & Dragon* and enviously watched the landlord cut a slice from one of his famous pies. There would be chunks of steak and knobs of kidney; there would be chubby circles of orange carrots, yellow cubes of parsnips and small transparent globes of onions lurking in the rich brown gravy that covered the meat. It was a pie to dream of!

'Out you go, all of you,' said the landlord firmly. 'No begging allowed here.'

Hastily Alfie took some coins from his pocket and held them out. He wanted to taste that pie so much that he just could not speak.

The landlord looked surprised. 'All right,' he said, his eye on the coins. 'How many slices?'

Alfie's voice came back to him. He stared at the perfect circle of the golden crust and knew what he must do. He put the copper coins back into his pocket, advanced to the counter and slapped two silver shillings down on to it.

'I'll take the whole pie,' he said triumphantly.

ACKNOWLEDGEMENTS

Much gratitude to all my family – my husband who accepts that trips to London will include quite a bit of research, my son who sets up and maintains my two computers, my daughter who is always full of such good suggestions for ways around difficult parts of the narrative, and my son-in-law who has made such a wonderful website for me.

Thanks to my junior editor, Peter Wall, who read the first one hundred pages and frankly acknowledged that he hadn't a clue as to the murderer. That was so helpful!

Thanks, also, to my agent Peter Buckman who is always so agreeable about reading and commentating on my books.

Anne Clark of Piccadilly has been the perfect editor, committed, involved and relentless in the quest to produce a good book. I owe her so much and am glad to have this opportunity to acknowledge my gratitude.

THE LONDON MURDER MYSTERIES

The MONTGOMERY MURDER

In the mean streets of Victorian London lies
the body of wealthy Mr Montgomery.
The police must move fast to catch his killer.
They need an insider, someone streetwise,
cunning, bold . . . someone like Alfie.

When Inspector Denham makes him an offer
he can't refuse, it's up to Alfie and his gang
to sift clues, shadow suspects and negotiate
a sinister world of double-dealing and danger –
until the shocking truth is revealed.

'A hugely enjoyable read . . . The characters are fun,
brave and resilient.' **Bookzone4boys**

THE LONDON MURDER MYSTERIES

MURDER ON STAGE

A scream rings out through the theatre. The man on stage is dead! Who killed him? Alfie has a few suspects in his sights.

But when the spotlight turns on Alfie himself, the search for the murderer becomes a fight for his own survival. He and his gang must pick their way through a deadly web of revenge, jealousy and greed to unmask the true villain.

COMING SOON

Find out more about the
𝒯ʜᴇ 𝓛ᴏɴᴅᴏɴ 𝓜ᴜʀᴅᴇʀ 𝓜ʏꜱᴛᴇʀɪᴇꜱ

www.piccadillypress.co.uk/
londonmurdermysteries